Nightmare

*Also by Joan Lowery Nixon
in Large Print:*

The Haunting

Nightmare

Joan Lowery Nixon

Thorndike Press • Waterville, Maine

Recommended for Young Adult Readers.

Published in 2004 by arrangement with
Random House Children's Books.

Thorndike Press® Large Print The Literacy Bridge.

The tree indicium is a trademark of Thorndike Press.

The text of this Large Print edition is unabridged.
Other aspects of the book may vary from the original edition.

Set in 16 pt. Plantin by Al Chase.

Printed in the United States on permanent paper.

Library of Congress Cataloging-in-Publication Data

Nixon, Joan Lowery.
    Nightmare / Joan Lowery Nixon.
      p. cm.
    Summary: Emily is sent to a camp for underachievers
where she discovers a murderer on the staff who might
provide an explanation for her recurring nightmares.
    ISBN 0-7862-6911-1 (lg. print : hc : alk. paper)
    1. Large type books. [1. Camps — Fiction. 2. Murder
— Fiction. 3. Nightmares — Fiction. 4. Mystery and
detective stories. 5. Large type books.] I. Title.
PZ7.N65Ni 2004
  [Fic]—dc22
                                2004051776

To Shirley Lyons,
a superior teacher,
who enriches her students
with the love of reading

CHAPTER 1

Shades and shadows slithered over and around her, trailing wisps of damp air, sticky-sweet honeysuckle, and the acrid smell of rotting leaves. Her heart pounded, and she grunted with exertion, struggling to get through the tangle of vines, knowing — even in her sleep — what she would find when she broke free. The crumpled body lay half in, half out of the water, eyes stretched wide with horror, mouth open in a scream no one could hear.

In her nightmare the body was always there.

Emily Wood's mother twisted, reaching from the front seat of the car to clutch Emily's knee. "Wake up, love," she said, her voice filled with concern. "You're having a bad dream again."

Emily gasped for breath as she opened her eyes to the overbright early-afternoon sun that flooded the car. In spite of the air-

7

conditioning, she was clammy with sweat, and her mouth felt dry and fuzzy. She struggled to sit upright, pushing back damp strands of the curly, pale hair that had fallen over her face, and willed the familiar nightmare to vanish from her mind.

Mrs. Wood's face sagged with worry. "Emily, if you would only tell us about the dream and talk about why it frightens you . . . perhaps if we found a good therapist —"

"It's only a stupid dream, Mom. It doesn't mean anything. I don't want to talk about it. I just want to forget it."

"But this nightmare has recurred ever since you were a little girl, and now you're sixteen — almost seventeen. Isn't it time that —"

"Mom! Please!"

Emily's father, Dr. Robert Wood, quickly glanced from the road, then back again. "Let it go, Vicki," he said softly. "We're almost there."

Mrs. Wood swung forward, ducking her head and burrowing her shoulders into the contoured padded leather of the passenger seat. "I was only trying to help her," she complained, as if Emily couldn't hear. "She has never let me help her. It's like her hair. If she just let me take her to a good stylist . . ."

Emily didn't respond. She was tired of

8

trying to explain to her mother that talking about it would make the nightmare more real. The bad dream had first popped into her mind, terrifying her, when she was much younger. Had she been eight? Ten? And every now and then it would unexpectedly reappear. The dead body . . . the blood on its face . . . the sickening smell of too-sweet honeysuckle blossoms. Emily was completely puzzled about the nightmare and what it might mean. She had never told anyone what she saw in the dream. She was sure she never would.

The car slowed and turned into a wide drive under an arched sign that read CAMP EXCEL.

Emily made a face. Camp *Excel?* Who did they think they were kidding?

Her mother sat upright and, in what Emily thought of as her let's-all-be-in-a-happy-mood voice, began commenting about the beautiful rolling hills and the bursts of gold black-eyed Susans and pale Queen Anne's lace that dotted the roadside. Her father added a few enthusiastic comments about the beauty of the Texas Hill Country in contrast to the flatness of Houston, but Emily slumped against the backseat, unable to believe what was happening to her.

It had been no surprise when teachers had labeled her an underachiever. The surprise was that anyone expected her to do any better. Her oldest sister, Angela, had aced every test she'd ever taken. She'd been valedictorian of her high school graduating class and was now among the top ten at Harvard Law School, planning some day to join their mother's law firm. Monica, next in line, was also valedictorian. She had chosen to follow in their father's medical footsteps and attended the University of Southern California, majoring in premed.

Angela and Monica gave speeches, led programs, and walked across stages to win honors and medals. The idea of trying to match what her sisters did, in rooms filled with eyes staring at her, terrified Emily. Content to disappear in any crowd and in any classroom, Emily was comfortable being little known and hardly ever noticed. She didn't even mind being classified as an underachiever, if that was what it took to be invisible.

Emily suppressed a sigh, wishing everyone would just leave her alone. It was plain bad luck that her tenth-grade guidance counselor had called her parents, excited about Camp Excel, a new, intensive six-week experimental summer program for students who were not performing to their abilities.

"It certainly wouldn't hurt to send you, darling," Mrs. Wood had announced at the dinner table. "Nothing else — rewards . . . tutors . . . praise . . . Nothing we've tried has helped." She had tucked a loose strand of her light, gray-streaked hair behind her ear and had smiled encouragingly at Emily. "According to Mrs. Carmody, Dr. Kendrick Isaacson has developed an absolutely marvelous summer program to help underachievers learn to do their best. He's gaining fame among both psychiatrists and educators."

"I never heard of him," Emily had said. "I bet you didn't, either, until Mrs. Carmody told you about him."

"Of course I have. His field is psychology. Patty Foswick, my friend in Dallas, has raved about him and urged me to take you there for an evaluation. But I realized that Dallas would be too far away for you to do any extended work with him, but in the Hill Country resort they're using for the summer school —"

Emily's father had interrupted. "Is he in private practice?"

"No," Mrs. Wood had answered. "He's one of the founders of the Foxworth-

11

Isaacson Educational Center in Dallas."

Emily had dropped her fork with a clatter, her fingers suddenly unable to hold it. For an instant she was numb, unable to see or breathe or think.

"Emily?" she'd heard her father ask from a long distance away. "Emily? Is something the matter?"

Gripping the edge of the table, Emily had forced herself to take a deep breath. As she'd felt her mother's hand clamp onto her forehead, she'd opened her eyes. "I — I'm okay," she'd said. "For a moment I just . . ."

She couldn't finish the thought. She had no idea why she'd suddenly felt a horrible fear rush through her body. It didn't make sense, so there was no way she was going to say anything to her parents about it. She'd repeated the words over again in her mind, *The Foxworth-Isaacson Educational Center.* Had she heard the name before? She had no recollection of it. So why had it made her so afraid? Emily could find no explanation.

"She isn't running a fever," Mrs. Wood had said, and had taken her hand away. "But did you see, Robert? The color absolutely drained from her face. I thought she was going to faint. Is there some new virus going around Houston?"

"Nothing out of the ordinary," he'd answered.

Emily had been aware that her father was studying her, so she'd refused to look in his direction. She'd deliberately picked up her salad fork and poked at the bits and pieces of pot roast and noodles on her plate, still puzzled by what had just happened.

Dr. Wood finally had asked, "Vicki, have you ever visited this educational center?"

"No," Emily's mother had answered. "But, as I told you, I've heard glowing things about it, even before now. Patty — you remember Patty. I went to school with her — used to live in the same neighborhood as the center. It's situated on a gorgeous old estate in Dallas. Patty raved about the progress Dr. Isaacson and Dr. Foxworth were making in getting kids back on track. I remember when Emily and I visited Patty and her daughter Jamie for a weekend years ago. Jamie had been nine or ten, about two years older than Emily, and —"

Panic grew like a tight knot, threatening to close Emily's throat. She'd wanted nothing to do with this educational center. She didn't know why. She'd only realized that she had to fight whatever her parents were planning. She'd interrupted her mother: "Nobody asked me if I wanted to go to this camp. Don't I have a choice?"

Emily's father had spoken firmly, probably the way he spoke to reluctant patients who balked at getting their shots, Emily guessed. "No," he said. "You don't."

"But, Dad, I don't need —"

"Emily," he had countered, "you *do* need."

"I can't."

"You will. If your mother and your guidance counselor think it's for the best, then it's for the best. There will be no more discussion about it."

Emily knew it would be futile to try to change her parents' minds, so she hadn't.

The car swung around a curve, and Emily's memories were broken by her mother's sudden exclamation of surprise. "This doesn't look like any summer camp I've ever seen," Mrs. Wood said. "It's beautiful. The pictures in the brochure don't do it justice."

"You told me the property once operated as a resort," Dr. Wood said. Then he mumbled under his breath, "It costs more than any resort," but Emily heard.

She glanced out at the low, gleaming two-story stucco buildings that formed a parenthesis around a wide expanse of neatly trimmed lawn. White gravel pathways, bordered with orange and yellow splashes of summer marigolds, connected the buildings. Through the open gap beyond the cozy circle lay the deep blue waters of a lake. The view was attractive. But Emily shuddered, and again she was puzzled by her fear.

Dr. Wood parked in an empty slot near the main entrance of the building on the left. "You made sure your suitcases had yellow tags on them, didn't you, Emily?"

"Yes, Dad," she answered. Why did he have to ask?

"Okay," he said. "Instructions were to stack all luggage behind the car where it could be picked up and delivered to the rooms." He climbed out of the car, carefully shutting the door behind him.

Before she left the car, Mrs. Wood reached back and gripped Emily's arm. "Darling," she said, "don't look so desperate. Everything here is going to be wonderful."

As Emily tried to relax and make her expression blank so that her mother couldn't read it, Mrs. Wood continued. "We'll be right here this afternoon for parent orientation. Right here with you, Emily." Her voice went up a cheerful notch. "And by the time we leave you won't even miss us because you'll have made some lovely new friends."

"And we can all go out and play," Emily muttered, even though she knew she wasn't being fair to her mother, who was only trying to help.

Sighing, Mrs. Wood left the car and Emily — knees wobbling — managed to climb out. *What is the matter with me?* she wondered as she leaned against the open door. *Why should I be so afraid?*

Trying to steady herself, Emily stood quietly, eyes closed, breathing in the sharp, acrid scents of sunbaked pine, marigolds, and newly cut grass.

"Come, Emily," she heard her father say. "The office is this way."

They entered a large, bright room that must have once been the lobby of the former hotel. It still looked like a hotel lobby, with groupings of sofas, tables, and high-backed chairs, and Emily wondered if the hotel furniture had been part of the sale.

The lobby was filled with teenagers and adults. The parents looked hopeful and somewhat intimidated, and they hovered near their offspring like hens with their chicks. The staff members were dressed in matching red polo shirts and khaki slacks or skirts, all so obviously brand new they looked like costumes in a play instead of leisure clothes. Smiles beaming and right hands extended, they greeted Emily and Dr. and Mrs. Wood, pulling them into the crowd.

After she had murmured countless hellos to faces she'd never seen before, and heard names immediately forgotten, Emily moved back against a wall. Leaving her parents to chat with some of the staff, she quietly studied the people in the room who were her own age.

They mostly looked like the kids in her high school in Houston, except for one tall guy whose shoulders curled down in a slouch and who wore a way-out-of-season wool knit cap pulled over his ears, and a girl whose long hair, gelled and sprayed into spikes, was dyed billboard yellow with a touch of pink. Her eyes were ringed with heavy mascara, and her lips were a slash of deep magenta.

Emily guessed that in the room there were at least a hundred high school kids and nearly double that in parents.

Before long, however, the parents were shepherded off somewhere for an orientation lecture. As soon as they'd left, a muscular guy wearing a snug T-shirt leaped up onto one of the tables and grinned at the kids.

"Hi," he said. "By this time I think I've said hello to each and every one of you personally, but in case you've forgotten my name, I'm Coach Ricky Jinks. You can call me Coach Jinks or Coach or Ricky Jinks or Ricky or anything you like. Just don't call me late for dinner."

No one laughed, but Coach Jinks's pep continued to bubble up and out as though he'd received a standing ovation. "During the next two days I'm going to sign you up for swim team and canoeing and volleyball and you-name-it, but right now they've given me the job of assigning you to your rooms and seeing that you get there in one piece." He eagerly looked around. "Any questions?"

No one responded.

"Okay, then," Coach Jinks said, his cheerfulness not lapsing for even a second. "I'll call out names, and you'll come up here and get your room keys. You'll be in the building across the courtyard. Your luggage should be in your rooms, so unpack and take a little time to get acquainted with each other, but be back here by five-thirty for dinner. Cook's barbecuing something — probably whatever roadkill he ran across while driving here. I hope nobody in this crowd is choosy."

18

As he jumped down from the table and began calling out names, Emily couldn't help making a face of disgust. Next to her a short girl snickered. "Six weeks of this?" she said, rolling her eyes. "Those are the kind of jokes my stepfather likes."

Emily took a good look at the girl. Her sleek, dark hair was long and cut straight across, and her eyes were a deep, intense blue. At odds with her neatly ironed, conservative white blouse and shorts, she wore dangly crystal earrings, a row of narrow silver bracelets on each arm, and an odd rocklike pendant on a silver chain around her neck.

The yellow-pink blonde Emily had noticed earlier moved a little closer. "He told me I belonged on his basketball team," she said quietly. "I hate basketball even more than I hate his jokes."

"Taylor Farris," the coach called, and the girl left, weaving her way to the front of the room.

The short girl rolled her eyes again and nudged Emily. "Can you believe that hair?" she whispered. "She is a decided hazard to what's left of the world's ozone layer."

"Haley Griffin," Coach Jinks called.

"That's me," the short girl said. She smiled at Emily. "See you later."

It took a few minutes to get to the last letters of the alphabet, but Emily waited patiently. She had nothing else to do. In a way it was satisfying to just stand back against the wall, unnoticed, and watch the others.

She jumped when she heard Coach loudly call, "Emily Wood."

Stumbling, she hurried to where he was stationed and waited while he checked off her name on his clipboard and handed her a plastic card. A hole was punched in one end, a cord through the hole. "You're in room 101," he said, studying Emily's face as if he were trying to memorize it. "Hang your key around your neck. That way you won't lose it."

He abruptly turned back to the clipboard and shouted, "Arthur Zimmerman!"

Emily hurried down one of the paths that led to the other building. She walked inside and followed the wall sign that listed the room numbers. Doors were open, talk and laughter pouring out, but Emily kept her head down, scurrying all the way to room 101, hoping no one would stop her or speak to her.

It didn't occur to Emily that she wouldn't have a room of her own until she stepped inside the open door of room 101 and saw a heap of clothes on one of the matching twin beds.

"This closet is definitely not big enough," a muffled voice complained just before Haley Griffin poked her head around the edge of the door.

"Hi," she said to Emily. "I guess we're going to be roommates. Your name's Emily Wood. Am I right?"

"Uh, r-right," Emily stammered, taken by surprise.

"Well, hang on until I get all my stuff into the closet," Haley said. She disappeared for a moment, then leaned back to look pleadingly at Emily. "I hope you don't need too much space. My mother got me all this stuff she claimed were the proper clothes for camp, but I brought some of the things I like to wear, too, like for when I meditate. You know."

Emily shook her head. "That's all right. I brought mostly T-shirts, shorts, and jeans. I can keep them in the chest of drawers."

"Actually, I think I filled up most of the drawers," Haley said. "You can have the bottom two. Okay?"

"Okay," Emily said quietly. She had never met anyone like Haley, but since she had to share a room with her for the next six weeks, she'd search for some quiet places around this camp where she could get away by herself.

Haley grinned at her. "There's just one more thing I have to do before we settle in."

"What's that?" Emily asked.

"Find out if there's anything interesting about you, Em," Haley answered.

Emily winced. "My name's *Emily*. Nobody's ever called me Em. And there's nothing interesting about me to tell."

"I'll decide that," Haley said. "Your father's a doctor, and your mother's a successful attorney."

"Wait a minute," Emily said. "How did you find —"

"Enrollment cards. In plain sight on Dr. Anderson's desk. But if they weren't, I'd find out anyway. I find out everything I need to know, and I'm going to find out all about you. And lucky you, you'll get to hear all about me."

"There's really nothing —," Emily tried again, but Haley interrupted.

"You probably want to be here just as much as I do, so lighten up. They may think they're going to get us to conform and study, study, study, but I have news for them. We're going to get together with some of the other kids and have fun."

Haley swung the door shut, then flopped

cross-legged onto the nearest bed. A wooden box, almost the size of a shoe box, slid out from under what was left of the pile of clothes next to her. Something inside it rattled.

"What's that?" Emily asked.

Haley's smile was smug as she motioned to Emily to join her on the bed. "My runes," she said, and hugged the box to her chest. "I wouldn't go anywhere without my runes."

Emily perched gingerly on the edge of the bed, fighting the urge to run from the room. She didn't want Haley for a roommate. She didn't want *anyone* for a roommate. She didn't want to be here in the first place. But, as her father had declared, she didn't have a choice.

"You didn't ask," Haley said.

"Ask what?"

"About my runes. Do you know what they are?"

Emily sighed. "No, I don't. Okay. What are runes?"

"They're my guide. My truth seeker. My power." Haley, still clinging to the box, slowly closed her eyes.

"You haven't really told me anything," Emily complained. "I still don't know what they are."

Leaning forward, Haley held out the pendant she was wearing. "This is a rune charm," she said. "It's not made out of rock, like the real rune stones. It's pewter, but it's enchanted for empowerment. The symbol on it is Feoh, which stands for wealth and good fortune."

To Emily the black symbol drawn on the charm looked like nothing more than a lopsided tree, bare of leaves, but she silently watched as Haley carefully laid the box between them and slowly opened the lid. Inside the box were small stones — about three dozen, Emily guessed. On each stone strange-looking symbols had been artistically drawn with black paint.

"Runes are part of a primitive alphabet that was developed by the Vikings well over two thousand years ago," Haley explained. "Somebody, I don't know who, found these alphabet symbols in caves throughout Scandinavia and discovered they had magic insight into the future." She leaned forward, her voice dropping as though she were imparting secret information. "Runes are probably the most powerful way of all to foretell the future."

Emily reached out to pick up one of the stones, wanting to examine it, but Haley gasped and pushed her hand away. "Not yet," she said. "We have to meditate."

"I just wanted to —"

Haley shook her head. "If you want to do this right, you *have* to meditate cross-legged for at least three minutes. You absolutely must sit cross-legged."

"But I —"

"Go on. Cross your legs," Haley insisted.

Emily sighed and did what she had been told.

"Now, close your eyes. Meditate."

"About what?"

Haley sighed impatiently. "About whatever people meditate about. Life, your aspirations, your hopes, your childhood. Okay?"

"I've never meditated before," Emily said. "I don't even know what meditation is all about." She knew it would be easier to just go along with whatever Haley said, but she was beginning to balk at being constantly told what to do.

Haley rolled her eyes again, then slipped on a look of exaggerated patience. "Meditation helps us withdraw from the stress around us and frees the brain to fully use its energy potential. Now, close your eyes."

"Tell me first, what has meditation got to do with your runes?"

Haley thought a moment, frowning and twisting her lips. Suddenly she sighed again.

"Don't make this so difficult. It's just what I said. Meditation frees your brain so the runes can pick up the messages they need. Okay?"

Emily decided to give up, since it was clear that Haley never would. "Okay," Emily said, and closed her eyes. She decided to meditate on the subject of why some people thought a bunch of little stones with drawings on them could possibly foretell the future. She wished she were home. She wished she were lying on the floor, one arm wrapped around her cat, Twizzles, as afternoon sun spilled through the window, creating a deep yellow patch across the floor. Twizzles purring in the soft silence, drowsy, sleepy . . .

"Time's up," Haley said, startling Emily so much that she jumped. "I'll go first so you'll see how to do it. With all the last-minute rush to get here I didn't have a chance to draw my rune for today."

Emily watched as Haley held the box high with her left arm, then reached in with her right hand and drew out a stone. She glanced at the design, which was like a *Y* with its stem twisted. "Yggdrasil," Haley said, looking pleased. "It represents a sacred tree from which all life springs and stands for new beginnings." She replaced the stone inside the box and laid the box on the bed in front of Emily.

"Obviously, I'm supposed to be where I am at this time and place," Haley explained smugly. "No matter that I didn't want to come. According to the runes, today is a day of new beginnings for me, which you can see is certainly true. Maybe things aren't going to be so bad here after all."

She replaced the stone, stirred all the stones with her fingertips, then again held up the box. "Go ahead, Em. Your turn."

"No, thanks," Emily said. "I really don't believe in all that —"

"If you don't, you should," Haley insisted. "Come on. We're going to be roommates, so in a way our fortunes are tied together. I'm curious about what the runes will tell you, even if you're not." She held up the box, moving it close to Emily's face. "Pick one."

It was easier to do what Haley wanted than argue about it, Emily decided. She reached into the box, fingering the stones. One had a tiny rough spot at one end. She closed her fingers around it and pulled it out. On one side of the little stone were three black dots, forming a triangle. With the symbol side up on the palm of her hand, she held out the stone to Haley, who made no move to take it.

Her eyes wide, Haley said, "I can't believe you drew that rune."

"Why?" Emily asked.

"It's the Loki rune." Haley took a deep breath and explained, "He's the Norse god of evil and treachery."

Emily wanted to laugh. "Don't look so worried. I'm not planning to do anything either evil or treacherous."

Haley just held out the box. The moment Emily dropped in the stone, Haley snapped the lid shut and fastened it. "I know you're not," she told Emily. "Drawing the Loki rune doesn't mean *you're* going to do evil. It means . . . well . . . it's a serious warning that forces of evil are working against you."

Emily couldn't help shivering. But she insisted, "What you've told me doesn't make any sense. A little stone can't tell my future."

Haley clutched the box again and looked to each side, as though she expected someone, or something, to be listening. "It's not the stone, silly. It's the power behind the symbol. It's the power of the runes. Don't ask me to explain how it works. It just does. It warned that you're in danger, Em. Believe it."

Emily gulped. "I don't," she said. "I

won't." In the silence she studied Haley's worried expression. "Anyhow, what could I do about it?"

"I don't know," Haley answered, her voice barely a whisper. "But I'll stick right by your side the rest of today. Tomorrow —" She broke off and suddenly smiled. "Tomorrow, of course, you'll draw again, and I'm sure you'll get a much better message."

"The warning's only good for today?"

Haley jumped off the bed and put the box on the shelf in her closet. "We don't know yet. But if you get a new message tomorrow, it means the warning is over."

Emily wished Haley had never opened her box of runes. Were there really forces of evil working against her? Had she sensed this herself when she'd been afraid? When she'd had the nightmares? *Don't be stupid,* she scolded herself. *You can't take a box of little painted stones seriously. Forget all about this dumb warning.*

Emily sighed, wishing that forgetting weren't so hard to do.

CHAPTER 2

At last! It's taken long enough. But now, after all these years, just as I had given up, I have a name to go with the face. Emily Wood. I'd almost stopped hoping to find her.

Emily Wood. Yes. She exists.

It was a shock to meet her, even more than I had imagined it would be. Oh, yes. I'd imagined it over and over again during the time in which I tried so hard to discover her identity.

Then suddenly, there she was, standing in front of me.

I covered my feelings well when we met. I didn't show how it had unnerved me. With all the activity and bustle of people arriving at the camp, I doubt anyone would have noticed anyway.

Did she recognize me? I don't think so. I've never been sure that she actually saw my face that day. I checked the position of those curved marble stairs over and over again. Not until I was at her level could I have been seen, and then the flash from my camera must have blinded her. She may have heard my words, but voices can easily be forgotten. And, after all, it was eight years ago. If she had seen anything, surely she would have spoken up at the time, and she didn't. She's hardly likely to speak up now.

I had no trouble recognizing her. Maybe it's because of that cloud of pale blond, almost white hair. It's certainly unusual enough to remember. At the time it reminded me of the puffball on a dandelion gone to seed.

It helped that her face has changed very little from childhood into the teen years. It's one I'd remember easily even without the photograph to assist me.

I'll phone Alice at the center and tell her to send the Carter file by express delivery. Alice won't ask why, and she won't snoop to see what's in the file. Alice never snoops. She is a highly professional secretary. I think she's simply lacking in basic curiosity. No matter. The photo of Emily Wood as a child is hidden in that file. I'm the only one who has ever seen that photograph.

If I can help it, I'm the only one who ever will.

CHAPTER 3

At the light tap on the door, Emily, who stood close by, opened it.

Before her stood the tall guy with the weird wool cap. It had been pulled even farther down over his ears than before. His nose was a little too long and his face too thin. His oversized, faded T-shirt and jeans hung on him as though he were nothing more than a stretched-out coat hanger. *If he had a nickname,* Emily thought, *it would have to be Bony or Skinny.*

His voice wobbled from high to low and back again as he said, "Hi. Maxwell McLaren here. I'm knocking on doors, getting acquainted."

"I'm Emily Wood," Emily said.

Maxwell nodded. "Any other mislabeled underachievers around here? Speak up now or suffer the consequences," he said.

Emily blinked. "*Other* mislabeled underachievers?"

"That's correct," Maxwell said. "I, for

one, have definitely been mislabeled. I am not an underachiever. I simply refuse to waste my time on subjects which will be of no use to me in my future, such as math and science."

Emily couldn't help giggling. Then, embarrassed, she quickly said, "I'm sorry. I shouldn't have laughed. It's just that . . ."

Maxwell didn't look hurt. He looked pleased. "Any response is better than no response," he said. "And since you seem to be vitally interested in why I'm not an underachiever, I'll tell you that I plan to become a highly respected, award-winning, very rich playwright someday. Are you going to dinner?"

Emily blinked, trying to follow the conversation. "Am I what?" she asked.

"Going to dinner," Maxwell said. "You'll meet your parents in the dining room. I saw you with them earlier. If you're ready, I'll walk over there with you now."

"I — uh —" Emily threw a quick glance toward Haley, hoping for help, but Haley, grinning wickedly, disappeared into the closet with her last armful of clothing.

Emily took a deep breath as she turned back to Maxwell. "How old are you?" she asked.

"My birth certificate would lead you to

believe that I'm fifteen," Maxwell said. "But my true age is light-years beyond that."

"Look, Max —"

"Maxwell," he interrupted. "Never Max. Maxwell is an old family name, and it's perfect for a playwright. Max is not."

"Okay, Maxwell, then," Emily said. "You wouldn't want me to walk to the dining room with you because then you wouldn't be able to find what you're looking for."

For an instant Maxwell seemed puzzled. "What am I looking for?" he asked.

"What you said — other mislabeled underachievers."

"Oh, that," he answered with a shrug. "I've decided to end my quest and concentrate on you. You're not exactly the most beautiful girl in the world, but your frizzy hair reminds me of cotton candy. I like it."

Emily kept herself from groaning aloud. Her mother was always complaining that her hair was frizzy and wanting her to do something about it, but Emily liked her hair the way it was. She could duck her head, letting a curtain of hair fall around her face, and when she wanted to she could hide behind it. Emily wished she could do that now. She didn't want to make friends with Maxwell or Haley or anyone else. She wanted to be left alone.

"It's time to go over to the dining hall," Maxwell said. "Some people have already left the dorm."

Emily tried again. "Thanks anyway, Max — uh, Maxwell, but I'm going to dinner with my roommate, Haley."

Maxwell brightened. "Fine. I'll walk with both of you."

Haley appeared at Emily's side. "Hi," she said. "I'm Haley Griffin. I heard you say you weren't really an underachiever."

"That's right," Maxwell said, and he repeated what he had told Emily.

As they walked down the hall, Emily envied Haley's ability to talk with a guy she had just met. Emily found it hard to make conversation with any of the guys at school, including those she'd known since kindergarten. But when they met up with some of the others who were staying in their dorm, Haley stopped to talk to them, and Emily was forced to talk to Maxwell.

"So, are you writing a play now?" she asked him.

"Not right now," Maxwell answered. "At the moment I'm walking with you to the dining hall."

Emily rolled her eyes. "You know what I meant."

"How can I know what you meant when

you didn't even know what you meant?"

"What are you talking about?" Emily asked.

"You didn't want to know about my play. You were just making conversation."

Emily looked down at her feet, which were crunching on the gravel path. She didn't know how to respond. She didn't have to.

"I come from a family in which you don't write plays, you play baseball and football and soccer," Maxwell continued. "Oh, yeah, and I shouldn't forget swim team. My big brother follows the family pattern and comes home with trophies. I don't. I don't even come home with straight A's to make up for it. So to my parents and teachers I'm an underachiever. Mislabeled, of course."

He looked down at Emily as he held the door to the lobby open for her. "How about you? Have you got any older brothers to bug you?"

"No brothers. Only two sisters, both older, and they do come home with straight A's."

"And you don't?" Maxwell asked.

"There you are, darling," Emily heard her mother call.

"See you, Maxwell," Emily said, relieved that she didn't have to answer the question.

She wasn't Angela. She wasn't Monica. She was *Emily*. Why couldn't anyone understand that?

Mrs. Wood stepped up, resting an arm around Emily's shoulders, and soon she had introduced herself and Emily's father to Haley and Maxwell, and their parents.

Some of the faces of staff members floated into view again as they stopped to speak. Emily realized that she was going to live with them for the next six weeks, so this time she tried to put names with faces and remember them.

Dr. Kendrick Isaacson himself . . . thick mane of white hair . . . smooth tan . . . dark, piercing eyes . . . teeth too white and perfect to be real. . . . He makes me feel like a bug on a microscope slide.

"It will be my ultimate satisfaction to see Emily and the other young people here strive for their highest potential," Dr. Isaacson announced to Emily's parents.

"Wonderful!" Emily's mother responded.

Emily suspected that Dr. Isaacson would make this same announcement over and over to every parent in the room. Did it really mean anything?

Dr. Lorene Anderson, the director's assistant . . . tall . . . slender . . . narrow-eyed, intense look on her face. . . . Is she always so super-

charged when she talks about the center, or is she putting it on for the parents?

"I'm an ardent fan of Dr. Isaacson's teaching methods," Dr. Anderson said to Emily's parents. "I've worked with him for years, and I'm eager for Camp Excel to succeed because we will all share in its success."

As Mrs. Wood murmured agreement, Dr. Anderson added, "Dr. Isaacson is on his way to becoming a major name in the field of education. Since you live in Dallas, you must be familiar with his work."

"We've never lived in Dallas," Mrs. Wood said. "We live in Houston."

Dr. Anderson smiled. "Please forgive me," she said. "I've obviously mixed you up with the Drake family. So many new faces and names to learn all at once."

Gary Anderson, math teacher . . . Dr. Lorene Anderson's husband. He's fairly good-looking for a guy who's obviously over forty, but the stink of cigarette smoke clings to his clothes. Mom read the rules aloud, so I know that smoking is forbidden on camp grounds. Mr. Anderson must sneak off now and then for a smoke. I wonder where.

"You've met my wife," Mr. Anderson said. "This camp's all she's been able to talk about for months."

"Have you worked with Dr. Isaacson long?" Mrs. Wood asked, and Emily wondered if her mother had also suspected that Mr. Anderson lacked his wife's enthusiasm for this summer job.

"Longer than some of the others," he answered. "That's how Lorene and I met — at the center."

Gail Comstock, history teacher . . . short brown hair, pug nose, and a face splashed with freckles. Wide smile. Does she ever get tired of smiling?

"I like working with kids," Mrs. Comstock said. Even though she seemed to be speaking to Emily's parents, her gaze never left Emily's face. "I expect the best of them, and I've always got an ear for their problems, if they want to confide in me."

Emily found herself moving a step closer to her mother. She had no intention of confiding in anyone, especially this teacher, who might be as interested as she claimed, but who was probably just nosy.

Dr. Lydia Hampton, counselor . . . reddish blond hair, gray streaked, pulled back into a tight twist . . . deep brown eyes.

"I'm intent on reaching into the psyches of these kids and helping them achieve success by breaking down the barriers that are holding them back," she told the Woods.

"It's a win/win situation, as it will be for all of us when Dr. Isaacson proves what this camp can do."

"Emily's had therapy," Mrs. Wood said hesitantly. "The therapist felt that since Emily's two older sisters have consistently excelled, Emily has compared herself unfavorably, and he was unable to . . ."

Her voice trailed off weakly, but Dr. Hampton stepped close and spoke decisively. "The younger child syndrome is quite common. We should have no problem with that."

We? Emily thought. *How did my problem get to be yours?*

Arthur Weil, English teacher . . . bald . . . skinny shoulders and a potbelly. I hope I'll never have to see him in a bathing suit.

Emily jumped when Dr. Weil leaned into her face and said, "We'll keep journals, Emily. Do you get that? We'll *keep* journals. We'll *write in* journals. We'll never, ever use the noun *journal* as a verb. People who use the English language correctly do *not* journal."

Emily nodded quickly. "Yes, sir," she answered, wondering what that was all about.

There were other names and faces, too many to remember. She was thankful when a dinner gong sounded, double doors were opened, and the group began flowing into a large dining room.

The tangy wood-fire smell of brisket and barbecue sauce was so strong that Emily's stomach rumbled in response. But there were introductions of the staff all over again, and as director and founder of the camp, Dr. Kendrick Isaacson gave a welcoming speech.

"Some have called my approach to underachievement radical," he said. "And I suppose it is. But radical or not, it works, and this summer we're going to prove to the world of education that it works. I've assembled teachers and counselors who wholeheartedly follow my plan, and your children are going to benefit." Modestly, he gave a little bow and added, "We're all going to benefit."

"Oh, I hope so!" Emily heard her mother whisper as the applause began.

Emily was glad when the speech was over and plates heaped with barbecued beef, potato salad, and cole slaw were quickly slapped down at every place by a group of waiters who must have been told to hurry.

The buzz of conversation rolled over the tables in waves, but Emily, eyes downcast, didn't talk. She had nothing to say that anyone would want to hear, so she just concentrated on her food, which was very good. At least mealtime during camp life wouldn't be too bad.

Emily went through the rest of the evening like an automaton. In and out of her ears bounced lists of rules and schedules, and she collected fistfuls of papers that she was either supposed to sign, read, or put into a special three-ring notebook with CAMP EXCEL and her name stamped on the beige cover in a dark greenish gold.

By the time parents were scheduled to say goodbye, Emily's numbness had turned to resentment. Clutching the notebook and papers to her chest as a bulky barrier to her mother's tearful hug, she said, "I hope you can see what a really great summer you've given me."

"Oh, Emily," Mrs. Wood answered. "Please don't take that attitude. We're trying to help you —"

Emily interrupted. "Six weeks. Six weeks of people prying into my mind, just to please my parents. You didn't do this to Angela or Monica."

"But they didn't need —"

Dr. Wood shook his head. "It doesn't do any good to argue with her, Vicki. Let it go. Someday Emily will look back at this experience and thank us for it."

Fighting off tears, Emily couldn't give up. "Oops, for a minute I forgot," she said. "Parents are always supposed to be right."

Mrs. Wood leaned forward and kissed Emily's cheek. "Goodbye, darling. We'll be back for you in six weeks, and we'll write often. Please write to us. We'll miss you terribly."

"Goodbye, Emily," Dr. Wood said, and he kissed her other cheek.

Emily stiffened and refused to look at her mother or answer her. She knew she was being hateful. Above all else she wanted to throw her arms around her parents and hug them and keep them with her, if only for a little while, but they were leaving her here for the summer, and she couldn't forgive them for that.

Silently, she watched her parents climb into their car and drive away. Only after they were out of sight did the tears come.

Emily heard the crunch on gravel as someone stepped up beside her, but she couldn't stop crying.

"If you keep that up, your eyes will be all red and puffy, and you'll look horrible," Haley said. "And you won't seem nearly as desirable to Maxwell McLaren in his fabulously gorgeous knit cap."

Emily's sniffle turned into a hiccup. She

couldn't help smiling.

Haley turned toward the main building. "Come on, Em," she said. "Everyone's supposed to meet in the auditorium for a get-acquainted program, which is probably going to be a real bore."

Emily shivered. She didn't want to be part of a get-acquainted program. She'd already met more people here than she really wanted to know. Why couldn't she just be left alone? "You go ahead," she told Haley. "I have to go wash my face."

"Are you sure you'll be all right?" Haley asked. "I mean, I keep thinking about the warning the runes gave you. Do you want me to go with you?"

"I'll be fine by myself. Go to the program," Emily insisted, eager to be alone.

She walked down the path toward the dorm, but as soon as Haley was out of sight and a few stragglers had also gone into the main building, Emily turned toward the lake. The beach lay before her, open to view by anyone at the buildings, but to her right lay a path that led into a stand of broad-limbed Spanish oak, where vine-draped limbs tangled with the twisted branches of madrone trees, blocking the camp buildings from sight.

Intent on being alone, Emily took the

path, quickening her pace until she broke through the tunnel of green to a small bay in the lake. At her feet lay the wooden planks of a short dock.

A faded red rowboat, tied loosely to a post at the end of the dock, bobbed up and down like a bathtub toy. Although the lake lay in shadow, with the low sun now hidden behind the surrounding forest, Emily walked to the end of the dock, her eyes on the dark ripples that flowed rhythmically across the lake from the river that fed it. The water was deep and peaceful. Emily began to relax, content to be alone.

She easily slipped into the comfortable silence, hearing only the soft lap of wavelets against the dock and an occasional creak of the aging planks. Across the expanse of water a few shore lights winked on and grew brighter as the sky gradually darkened.

It took a while for Emily to become aware that she was no longer alone. She had heard no sound, nothing that would make her believe that someone had approached. But she sensed that she was being watched. Eyes seemed to bore into her back. Someone was behind her. Hidden. She could feel it.

Emily turned, peering into the lowering dusk. "Who's there?" she whispered.

No one answered.

CHAPTER 4

I made time to scout out this part of the camp grounds, and came across a spot that is totally hidden from anyone on the path. Coach Jinks did not know that I watched him make some repairs on the old dock. Yet I was very near. At the time I had no idea that my hiding place would become useful for stalking Emily Wood.

When I spoke to her this evening, I searched her eyes but found no recognition there. She hasn't responded to my name or to my face. So why do I consider her a threat?

Because I do not know how much Emily remembers.

She's standing alone at the end of the dock. It's rocky there and deep. There's a possibility that she could fall into the lake and not come up. An accident. No one would think otherwise. Then the worry of what she might say or do would cease to exist.

But is it necessary?

I don't know yet.

She's turned. She's searching the area. She seems to realize that she's not alone here. I dare not move.

If I were to appear, blocking her path . . .

Not yet. Something tells me not yet. I must bide my time. Wait and watch. I'll need more information before I decide what to do about Emily Wood.

CHAPTER 5

"Who's there?" Emily repeated.

The silence became as absolute as someone holding his breath, and for a moment Emily froze, tiny droplets of cold sweat trickling down her spine.

Suddenly the small crack of a twig breaking snapped the silence, ending the spell.

Emily panicked, running back into the tunnel that snaked through the tangle of vines and branches. Stumbling, tripping over an exposed root, scraping her hands on rough bark as she flung herself against the support of a tree, somehow she managed to follow the path to the clearing and break free.

She abruptly stopped, bending over, arms stiffly braced on her knees while she sucked in loud gulps of air.

"Em?"

The voice was behind her, and Emily whirled. In terror she tried to scream. Her mouth opened, but the only sound she could make was a strangled gasp.

"What's the matter with you?" Haley stepped forward, grasping Emily's shoulders. "What happened? Why are you acting like this?"

Emily sagged against Haley's strength, then straightened, taking a long, deep breath. "You scared me," she said. "I didn't see you or anyone else. I didn't know you were there."

"Hey, *you* scared *me*. I had no idea where you were," Haley answered indignantly. She dropped her arms and stepped back, looking at Emily accusingly. "I promised to keep an eye on you. Remember? Because of Loki's warning. But then you sneaked away."

"I didn't sneak."

"You *did* sneak. You said you were going to wash your face and you'd be right back. But you didn't come back."

Emily saw Haley's expression change as she studied her. "Something scared you," Haley said. "What was it?"

"Part of my nightmare," Emily blurted out without thinking.

"What nightmare?"

She barely even knew Haley, but she was so unnerved she was unable to stop talking.

"Sometimes I have this nightmare. Not very often, but when it comes it's always the same. There are trees and honeysuckle vines, and I'm trying to get through them, and . . ."

Emily halted in midsentence. Why was she telling Haley all this? She didn't even like her that much.

Haley impatiently asked, "And what?"

Emily didn't want to tell the rest. She didn't want to even think about it. The tree limbs that brushed her face, the vines that tangled around her, her struggle to get through them, the strong fragrance of honeysuckle . . . At least this time there had been no body, no staring eyes, no blood. Emily put her hands to her head. It was beginning to ache.

"Go on. And what?" Haley repeated.

"That's all there is," Emily said.

"That's your nightmare?"

Emily brushed her hair from her eyes. "I don't want to talk about it, Haley. Let's talk about something else."

"Okay. Come back to the meeting. We've broken up into discussion groups. What for, I have no idea. I mean, I already know who I want to talk to and who it would be totally useless to know, like Pink Hair."

Emily sighed. She was glad for the

moment that Haley had appeared when she did, but Haley was a snob. "Her name is Taylor, not Pink Hair," Emily said.

Haley shrugged. "Whatever." She glanced in the direction of the lake and the finger of forest that crept down to meet the water, then took a step toward the lighted main building. "Let's not stay out here in the dark. *You* may not take the Loki warning seriously, but *I* do."

Emily didn't need Haley's urging. She wasn't positive that someone had been in the forest watching her. Maybe it had only been her imagination. Or perhaps a small animal caused the twig to snap. In any case, her desire to be alone was gone. She needed to be with other people.

They entered the meeting room to the hubbub of squeaking folding chairs, the thud of shoes hitting the wooden floor, and bodies up and in motion. The warm air was heavy with the leftover scent of barbecue, stale sunblock lotion, and someone's overdose of aftershave.

"Time to change groups, girls," Coach Jinks said. He gestured toward two empty chairs, and Emily soon found herself sent to one group, Haley to another.

Taylor scooted her chair two inches to the right to make room for Emily. "Cool hair," she said to Emily. "Where'd you find that almost white shade?"

"I was born with it," Emily said.

"No kidding? Cool. I mean *really* cool." Taylor reached out and gently touched Emily's hair with her fingertips. "It's so curly. That's why it stands out like that. It makes me think of one of those little soft clouds that hangs all alone in a hot summer sky."

Taylor's words were like something from a greeting card, but her smile was so earnest, Emily smiled back easily. "Thanks," she said.

A woman who wasn't as tall as the kids around her stirred on her folding chair, raising her voice. "Okay, everybody. Time to settle down. We're supposed to be getting acquainted."

Emily glanced from the woman, whom she had met earlier as Maria Jimenez, the camp nurse, to the others seated in their tight circle.

"I'm Mrs. Jimenez," the nurse continued. "I'm on the spot if you get sick or hurt, which you won't if you use good common sense, eat properly, and get enough sleep."

One of the guys gave a snort, and a couple of the other guys in the circle laughed.

"I guess there's always gotta be a wise guy," Mrs. Jimenez said. "But the rest of you, take what I said seriously. You don't need to live on pizza or stay up all night talking, or try to show how macho you are and do dumb things like dive where there are rocks."

She deliberately turned to look at the boy who had snorted as she said this, and again there were a couple of snickers.

He scowled, but Mrs. Jimenez smiled at him. "Let's start with you, big boy," she said. "Tell everyone your name and where you're from and something about yourself."

His scowl grew deeper, and his voice came out in a low growl. "I'm Stan Keller. I live in Waco."

"How about what you like to do, Stan? Football? Weight lifting?"

The scowl disappeared, and Stan sat up a little straighter. "Football," he answered. "I'm a letterman, going into my senior year."

"What else do you do?" Mrs. Jimenez asked.

Stan's mouth opened in surprise. "I told you. Football," he said. "What else is there?"

Mrs. Jimenez nodded to the girl on Stan's left. "Okay, next," she said. "Let's hear about you."

"I'm Tammy Johnson," the girl said in a

voice barely above a whisper. "I live in Wichita with my parents and two brothers and a dog named Blooper —"

"Blooper! That's a stupid name for a dog," Stan interrupted.

"It's Tammy's turn now," Mrs. Jimenez told Stan.

Tammy seemed to shrink in her chair, but Taylor spoke up. "I think Blooper's a cute name."

Stan looked pointedly at Taylor's hair. "I don't think you'd know the difference between cute and weird," he said.

Mrs. Jimenez gave Stan a sharp look. "Dr. Isaacson's really big on self-esteem," she said. "It would be nice if we'd all think about what we're going to say before we say it."

"I don't think I look weird," Taylor said. "I'm choosing to be myself, not a clone of everyone else."

One of the guys seated across the circle from Taylor spoke up. "My sister went for blue hair. She said it expressed her mood. But she was really just bugging our mom, who hated it."

"What my mom thinks about my hair doesn't matter," Taylor said.

"Bet she argues with you about it. Right?"

"She argues about everything I do. What

difference does it make?"

Mrs. Jimenez shrugged. "We're getting way off the subject. Right now let's think about the self-esteem of the people in this circle. Tammy, what else do you want to tell us about yourself?"

"There's nothing more to tell," Tammy said, staring down at the floor. "You can go on to someone else."

Emily could sympathize with Tammy, who obviously hated being singled out. She felt as if she were looking at herself.

"Why don't you tell us about your hobbies?" Mrs. Jimenez asked Tammy.

"They're nothing special," Tammy whispered. "Nobody would be interested. Please go on to someone else."

Mrs. Jimenez's glance fell on Taylor. "Okay, next. Please tell us your name and where you're from and something about yourself."

"Taylor Farris," Taylor said promptly. "I live in a suburb of Dallas with my mom, who's a legal secretary. My dad lives in Florida with his trophy wife, who's nine-tenths the result of plastic surgery. Mom made Dad pay my tuition for this camp, which I'm sure he did out of guilt."

Taylor took a deep breath, ready to continue, but Mrs. Jimenez interrupted. "What are your hobbies, Taylor? What do you like to do?"

Emily expected Taylor to say something about hanging out with her friends, so she was surprised when Taylor said, "I write poetry. It's good, too. My English teacher said so." Her upper lip curled in a sneer that she sent in Stan's direction.

Emily's smile disappeared as she realized Mrs. Jimenez was looking at her.

"Your turn," Mrs. Jimenez said.

"Emily Wood. I'm from Houston," Emily answered.

"Please speak up, Emily. I can't hear you over here," Mrs. Jimenez told her.

Emily repeated what she had said, forcing herself to talk loudly. Embarrassed as everyone in the circle looked at her, she bent her head, tucking in her chin and letting her hair drop like a curtain, shutting them off.

"Cool," Taylor whispered.

But Mrs. Jimenez said, "We want to know something about you, Emily. Do you take ballet? Do you sing?"

"No," Emily whispered.

"Are we having a talent show?" one of the guys in the circle asked eagerly. "I've got a comic routine that's pretty funny."

The guy next to him guffawed. "Where've you been, man? Haven't you been listening

56

to anything we're saying?"

"Not so you'd notice," Stan answered for him, and his group burst into laughter.

"Okay, settle down," Mrs. Jimenez said. "We'll go on to you, Paul. Tell us about yourself."

This time Emily decided not to listen. She didn't care what any of these kids were named or where they lived. She didn't want to be at this camp, but she had no way of leaving. She couldn't walk back to Houston. Even if she did risk it, her dad, who felt strongly that every project should be seen to its proper conclusion, would only bring her back to camp.

It was soon time to change circles and meet new people. Resentfully, Emily plopped herself into a folding chair next to Arthur Weil, the English teacher of the skinny legs and potbelly. When it was her turn to introduce herself, she fumbled through an answer to "Tell us your goals in life."

"I don't have any yet," she mumbled.

"You mean you haven't *defined* your goals yet," Dr. Weil said.

"No, I mean I haven't even thought about them."

"Then maybe it's the right time to begin doing so," he said, blinking and bobbing his head just like the owls at the Houston zoo.

Dr. Weil turned to someone else, and Emily again retreated behind her hair.

By the third change of circle Emily had stopped hating what they were doing and had settled into a numb complacency, even consciously listening to some of the people around her. A few of them gave interesting answers, like Raúl, who was destined to work in his father's bakery, but who really wanted to be a parachutist; and Karen, who dreamed of a job inventing new ice cream flavors for Ben & Jerry's.

As Emily joined the fourth circle, Maxwell slumped into the chair next to her. "We were destined to meet sooner or later," he said. "Have you been baring your soul?"

"I didn't come here to bare my soul," Emily told him.

"But that's what they have us doing, isn't it?"

"Not if we don't answer."

Maxwell smiled. "I like to answer," he said. "I like to answer in such detail that the facilitators have a hard time shutting me up."

Emily couldn't keep from smiling back. "What's a facilitator?" she asked.

"An important word for the members of the staff who have been assigned one to a circle. I wonder what question we'll be asked at this one."

They didn't have to wait long to find out. Gail Comstock, the history teacher, smilingly gazed around the group and said, "Now we're going to have fun reaching back in time. After you've introduced yourself, tell us about one of your childhood memories, perhaps when you were school age — six or seven."

A sudden blast of cold sliced through Emily's body. Shivering, she managed to get to her feet and said, "I'm leaving."

Mrs. Comstock's eyes widened. "Are you ill?"

"Yes . . . no, just cold," Emily said. She shivered again. "Maybe it's the air-conditioning."

"Please stay with us, Emily," Mrs. Comstock said. "This is our last get-acquainted circle of the evening."

"I'm really tired," Emily said, but, as though she had no control over what she was doing, she found herself sitting back down.

Mrs. Comstock leaned forward and patted Emily's shoulder. "Just take it easy, dear," she said. "We'll skip you for now and begin with this nice tall young man. Your name is Maxwell, isn't it?"

Maxwell bent his head in a low bow, then said, "Make note of this moment. Someday you will look back on it and say, 'That's when I actually met the famous playwright Maxwell McLaren.' "

One of the girls in the circle giggled, and Maxwell said to her, "Look me up when you visit New York in twenty years — no, make it ten — and I'll give you a pair of passes so you can see that my predictions were right. Don't expect the best seats, though. You'll be in the last row of the top balcony."

Mrs. Comstock chuckled. "If she doesn't take you up on that, I will," she said. "But for now, in the short time we've been given, we're dealing with early memories, not our hopes for the future."

"Very well," Maxwell said. "My earliest memory was when I was born. It was not a pleasant experience, but at the time I realized it was a necessary step and I'd have to endure it."

At this, everyone laughed.

"It's impossible to remember that far back," one of the guys said.

Maxwell shrugged and grinned in return. "Impossible for you, maybe, but not for me. Did I mention that when the doctor put his finger into my mouth to make sure it was cleared out, I tried to bite him? Unfortunately, I had no teeth."

Mrs. Comstock rolled her eyes, but she didn't stop smiling. "Thank you, Maxwell," she said, and turned her gaze to the girl on Maxwell's right. "How about you, Lauren? Want to go next?"

Lauren introduced herself, then giggled. "I remember a time when I was eight years old and visiting my grandparents and . . ."

Counterclockwise, they went in turn. Emily only half-listened, steeling herself to participate when her turn came. *If I do what she says I can get out of here,* Emily thought. *If I don't, it all just becomes more complicated.* She searched her brain for a memory and nearly sighed aloud in relief as one came to her.

Finally, Mrs. Comstock said, "Emily Wood, who's from Houston."

Emily closed her eyes for a moment, opened them, and said, "When I was in second grade there was a boy in my class named Kevin. He was always clowning around. He liked to scoop a goldfish out of our teacher's aquarium when she was out of the room and hold it up, pretending to swallow it. Some of the girls in the class would always squeal. Anyhow, one day he was holding the goldfish up by the tail over his open mouth when the fish gave a big wiggle and slipped through Kevin's fingers, and he accidentally swallowed it. We all fell on the floor laughing, but Kevin got in big trouble with our teacher."

The other kids smiled, but Mrs. Comstock said gently, "That wasn't a memory about your own life, Emily. It was *Kevin's* memory. Can you tell us something that *you* remember about your own childhood?"

Emily felt the back of her neck grow cold, and driblets of sweat shivered down her backbone. "Why?" she asked.

"Early memories are often keys to our present problems," Mrs. Comstock said. "Like keys, they can open doors."

"I don't have any problems," Emily insisted. She could feel herself trembling and wondered if the others could see it.

Mrs. Comstock said pleasantly, "Dear, this recall of early memories is a technique Dr. Isaacson has found to be very helpful. Maybe, if you just sit back and relax, something will —"

"No!" Emily shouted, jumping to her feet. "I can't!"

She pushed over her chair, which clattered to the floor, and ran as fast as she could away from the meeting room and everyone in it.

CHAPTER 6

I like these after-session discussions. They're worthwhile. All of us on the staff pool our knowledge of the young people in our care. We share our notes, observations, and insights, which helps us understand them better.

Of course, at the moment I think this sharing will help me particularly.

I desperately need to understand Emily Wood.

Her outburst and refusal to delve into her early memories became an immediate focal point in our staff discussion. Most of the staff are puzzled about the apparent fear that accompanied her flight from the discussion circle.

I'm the only one who suspects why Emily behaved in such a manner. And now I'm confronted by some serious questions.

Are Emily's memories still so real and frightening that she cannot deal with them? Or has she suppressed her memories so that they no longer exist?

If she has suppressed them, then the question that concerns me most is, Will these memories ever fully return? And if so, what will Emily do about them?

What did she see and hear?

What does she remember?

Can I afford to wait for the answer?

CHAPTER 7

Emily sat outside the main building, huddled inside a protective pool of light that shone from one of the large windows. She was too frightened to walk alone to her room in the empty dorm.

Suddenly a noisy mix of voices and bodies erupted into the lounge behind her and flowed through the main doors. Emily jumped to her feet, turning so suddenly that she nearly collided with Maxwell. He grabbed her arms, steadying her.

"I — I'm sorry," Emily stammered.

"Don't be." He studied her face, obviously puzzled. "Why'd you run out of the room?"

"I don't know," Emily said.

"You have to know. It was your decision."

"It wasn't a decision. I mean, it's not like I thought about it and decided to do it. I just felt like I had to get away."

Dr. Hampton pushed through the people

who were still clustered around the door. She stood in front of Emily, holding out a few sheets of paper. "You left too soon," she said. "Here's your schedule for tomorrow, Emily. On the back is a map of the area to help you find your way around the grounds and buildings. There are also a few forms for you to fill out."

Emily took the papers silently but didn't attempt to look at them.

Dr. Hampton rested a hand on Emily's arm and asked, "Is everything all right?"

"Yes," Emily said, flinching from Dr. Hampton's deep gaze. She knew that Dr. Hampton wanted her to explain why she had run from the meeting, but she couldn't. She didn't understand her own actions or the fear that churned inside her.

Haley popped into the group, stepping between Dr. Hampton and Emily. Giving a dramatic sigh as she waved her fistful of papers, she said, "We've got to fill all these things out, and I suppose it will take most of the night."

Without another word Dr. Hampton eased back into the stragglers who dawdled at the end of the flow from the building. Once again Emily was thankful for Haley's arrival on the scene. Dr. Hampton's gaze was like a probe, plunging and searching through the eyes into the mind, and Emily didn't want anyone to poke into her mind.

"Let's walk down to the beach," Maxwell suggested.

Haley strained to look at her wristwatch. "There's a curfew, doofus," she said. "We're supposed to be in our rooms in ten minutes. Besides, it's too dark."

"Sometimes I like to sit on the roof of our house in the dark after the whole world is asleep," Maxwell said. "It's the best time to think; nobody's there to bother me."

Haley looked interested. "Do you look up at the stars and meditate while you're on your roof?"

"No," he said. "I think about what it must be like to live in New York in an apartment overlooking Central Park and to take a limo to the theater where people applaud when they see me arriving."

Haley sighed. "Come on, Em. Let's get over to the dorm before we're the only ones left outside."

Emily threw a quick smile to Maxwell and hurried to follow Haley.

As soon as they were inside their room, with the door locked and lights bright, Haley leaned against the door and sighed with relief. "Whatever Loki warned about did not come to pass," she said.

Braver now that the day was nearly over, Emily said, "That should prove that a little stone can't foretell the future."

Haley shook her head stubbornly, her dark hair flying. "You're missing the point, Em. You were warned to take care, which means that Loki understood the evil that could be directed against you. Whoever was going to perform that evil, however, either changed his mind or was diverted in some way. Loki has no influence in that direction, so he can't be held responsible for a change of plans."

"Oh, honestly, Haley," Emily said. "I can't believe you're giving so much power to a box full of stones."

Haley flopped down on the bed and tossed her papers on the floor. "I told you, the stones are not important. It's the Norse symbols that are painted on the stones. They could be painted on paper or clay or buttons or anything you can think of. Remember, this system of foretelling the future through runes is two thousand years old."

As though she were speaking patiently to a child who had trouble paying attention, Haley added, "Tomorrow we'll pick our runes again. Whichever you draw, I'll help you interpret it."

"Okay," Emily said, the easiest way of ending the conversation. Suddenly she was exhausted, ready for sleep. The sooner she finished filling out the forms and going over her schedule, the sooner she could get to bed. She chose one of the matching desks, sat down, and reached for a pen.

A short time later she was sound asleep, covers pulled over her head, while Haley was still banging drawers open and shut, trying to find her pajamas.

It was very late, with the thin moon unable to light the sky and the smothering darkness thick and heavy with summer heat, when the nightmare came. In the hush, broken only by the soft sound of breathing, Emily struggled through a tangle of damp vines, peeling from her arms and legs the wet, clinging, rotting leaves. She gasped for air as she climbed toward the opening, terrified at what she knew was coming. Unable to help herself, she screamed as she again stared into the dead eyes of the pale, bloody face.

With a gasp Emily sat up in bed, sweating, shaking, the face indelibly imprinted on her mind. Had she cried out?

In the twin bed Haley murmured and rolled over, her sleep seemingly uninterrupted.

Emily took a few deep breaths, puffing them out through open lips, willing her rapid heartbeat to slow. No one had come running, and she hadn't awakened Haley, so the scream must have been only in her dream. She began to relax.

Through the dull glow that came through the window from the spotlights that surrounded the building, shadows in the room began to take the familiar shapes of dresser, desks, and chairs. Emily climbed out of bed and made her way to the bathroom. Without turning on the light, she washed her face with cool water and rubbed it dry.

Now that she was fully awake, it was easier to think. Over the years the nightmare had reappeared, but not very often. Yet lately it had been hounding her. Why? she wondered. What did it mean? Who was the woman in her nightmare?

Emily rested her forehead against the cold hardness of the mirror, closed her eyes, and whispered aloud, "What do you want of me?"

There was only silence.

When the bell rang at six the next morning, Emily struggled from a sleep that clogged her brain like a thick fog and wouldn't let go. As she brushed her hair, squinting toward the mirror, Haley squirmed past, strewing clothing to either side.

"Time to meditate and pick our runes before we go to breakfast," she said.

"Not today," Emily complained. "I'm not ready."

"Of course you're ready," Haley said. She grasped Emily by the wrist and led her to the rumpled bed. "Sit," she ordered.

Too tired to argue, Emily sat cross-legged on the bed.

Haley, clutching the box of runes, sat facing her. She gently shook the box, then opened it and laid it between them.

"Now close your eyes. Meditate on . . . um . . . I know. Meditate on what you hope to be someday."

Emily closed her eyes. Her ambitions went no further at the moment than simply hoping to fully wake up, so she didn't even try to meditate. She allowed herself to slide off into a doze.

Her eyes flew open with a start as Haley rattled the box of stones near her nose. "I'll go first again," Haley said. "It's much easier to take care of myself before I begin worrying about you."

She drew a stone with two parallel lines

slanted toward the right and seemed pleased. "Parjuk," she announced. "He's the rune of travel."

"Does that mean you're going somewhere?" Emily asked, hoping that Haley would.

"It can be interpreted in a number of ways," Haley told her. "It might mean the shopping trip we're taking into town this afternoon. Oh, I meant to tell you. I signed you up, too. On the other hand, it can symbolize following a new direction on the path of life." Smugly, she added, "We'll just see what comes about."

She thrust the box over Emily's head. "Draw your rune," she ordered.

Emily raised her right hand and thrust her fingertips into the box. She pulled out the first stone she touched and held it toward Haley on her flattened palm.

Haley gasped as she stared at the stone. "Loki!" she whispered. "Not again. It's never supposed to happen like that."

Emily quickly dropped the stone back into the box, shaken in spite of her nonbelief. "It probably felt familiar and that's why I chose it. It's just silly coincidence," she said.

"It's not coincidence. It's a grave warning."

"It's only a stone."

"It's a powerful rune."

"It's a stone."

"It's a warning that forces of evil are working to harm you." Haley hugged the box to her chest and stared wide-eyed at Emily. "We have to do something about this."

Emily sighed. Although fortune-telling by means of little painted stones made no sense at all, she couldn't help picking up Haley's fear. "What can we do?" she asked.

Haley's answer was immediate. "Find out if a *curandero* is in town."

"What is a *curandero*?"

"It's a person, a folk healer. Most live in the valley, but there are some in central Texas and in the Hill Country. I'll find out. If there is a *curandero* in Lampley, I'll know."

Emily had no doubt about Haley's ability to find out whatever it was she wanted to know, but she wasn't going to allow her roommate to drag her to a folk healer without learning exactly what a folk healer might do. "What will this *curandero* do about Loki?" she asked.

"Not do about *Loki*," Haley answered, "do about *you*." She nodded, content with her answer. "He'll find a way to protect you, maybe with a spell or maybe with something from his herb shop. It could be you need a purification rite or a protective charm."

"Maybe I need to just forget your little stones and go on about my life the way it was before I heard about runes."

Haley slid off the bed and tucked the box of runes away in the closet. "You can be as negative as you wish," she said. "It doesn't matter. It's a nuisance for me, but I have vowed to protect you."

The jangle of another electronic bell vibrated through the silence, and Emily stood, ready to leave for the dining room. The combination of the silly Loki stone and her recurring nightmare was enough to make anyone jumpy, but Haley's crazy idea about protection from a folk healer was too much to take. "Why can't we just go sightseeing and shopping in Lampley and forget about *curanderos*?" she asked.

Haley's smile was that of someone used to getting her own way. "Let's go to breakfast," she responded.

First on Emily's morning schedule of classes was a history elective with Mrs. Gail Comstock. Wary because of Mrs. Comstock's repeated invitation to share confidences, Emily kept her distance and found a seat in the back row.

She was surprised when Taylor sat next to her and reached out a finger, twisting a flyaway tendril of Emily's hair around it. "Did you comb it this morning?" she asked.

"Sort of," Emily said. "I brushed it, at least."

"Wow! It's all over the place. It's spectacular, actually," Taylor said.

Maxwell stretched his long legs over both Taylor's and Emily's and managed to reach the seat on the other side of Emily. He plopped down, tugging his wool cap even farther over his ears. "History is a meaningless collection of dates," he said. "Totally worthless. Does it matter if Columbus discovered America in 1492 or 1942? What matters is the present. We are here and now in the twenty-first century — what is taking place to enrich, protect, or ensure our lives today?"

"You give me a headache," Taylor told him.

"Better me than our illustrious teacher," Maxwell said. He looked at Emily beseechingly. "You understand, don't you?" he asked. "How can we care — really care — about a date or a battle or a treaty? They're meaningless moments, lost in a time we are well rid of."

At that moment Mrs. Comstock strode into the room, her short brown hair bouncing on her neck. "Come to order, please," she said. She took a silent roll, looking up and down the rows to find the students, then laid her roll book on a nearby chair. Emily was surprised to realize that no teacher's desk was in the room.

"This class is not going to be a testing ground in which we see how many dates we can memorize," Mrs. Comstock said. "Dates are convenient hooks on which we can hang our memories of events. But history is all about people — people like you and me who did things to change the world, sometimes for better, sometimes for worse. We're going to spend six weeks learning about people and why they did the things they did. That's history."

Maxwell raised one eyebrow as he glanced at Emily. "This class may have potential," he said, "*if* she means it."

"The Longhorn Cavern is not far from here. It's a state park that's open to the public," Mrs. Comstock continued. "The cavern is part of a series of caves that may stretch for hundreds of miles underground through the Hill Country and central Texas. Tomorrow we're going on a field trip to visit the cave, but today we're going to talk about the people who used it for their own benefit. Many years ago Comanche Indians used one of the large rooms for their council meetings. During the Civil War the Confederate army set up a manufacturing plant for gunpowder in the same large room, and later the cave was a hideout for a pretty wicked Texas outlaw named Sam Bass, who also used the cave to hide the gold he stole in train and bank robberies."

Taylor spoke up, and Emily could hear the tremor in her voice. "Do we really have to go down into a hole in the ground?"

"There are stairs and handrails," Mrs. Comstock answered. "And you can walk upright for most of the way. There's just one low stretch called Lumbago Alley."

She laughed, but Taylor shuddered and whispered to Emily, "I don't want to go underground. It's like being buried alive."

"No, it's not," Emily whispered back, but she could tell that Taylor wasn't listening.

Someone in the front row raised a hand. "I've never been in a cave," she said. "Will we have to fight off bats?"

Mrs. Comstock smiled. "There are a few bats and some tiny cave mice, but either they're in hibernation or they'll stay out of your way. There are well-defined paths and electric lighting."

The girl gave a sigh of relief. "So the cave is perfectly safe," she said.

"I didn't say that," Mrs. Comstock answered. "There are deep drops and danger spots if you stray off the paths, and slippery places you'll be told to avoid. Follow the rules, and nothing should go wrong."

Only if Loki stays away, Emily thought. Startled, she scolded herself mentally for even thinking of Haley's silly rune stones. Were the warnings going to color everything she did at this camp? Not if she could help it.

During the rest of the morning Emily attended an English course taught by Arthur Weil, who rhapsodized about the joys of diagramming sentences.

"Gross," Haley whispered to Emily, and Emily at first agreed, but by the time Dr. Weil had begun diagramming sentences from bad movie dialogue, looking for hilarious flaws, everyone in the class was laughing.

After a couple of lines from low-budget films, he went into dialogue they'd recognize from some blockbusters. On the board he wrote, "Ben Affleck in *Armageddon*: 'Well, we all gotta die, right? I'm the guy who gets to do it saving the world.' "

"He may be a star," Haley said, "but his dialogue isn't."

"The writer is responsible for the dialogue in the script, not the stars," Dr. Weil answered. "They just say the words. I'm betting that each of you can write better than many writers for movie actors do."

He cleared his throat, then said, "I want each of you to come up with an original creative writing project. You may write a poem, a play, a detailed book report . . . something that is of your own creation."

"How many words?" someone asked.

"It doesn't matter. It just must be original and as creative and interesting as you can make it. Everyone understand?"

There was a general murmur of agreement; then Dr. Weil went on to another topic.

Emily was surprised when the bell rang. She had actually enjoyed the class. She hadn't had to hide behind her hair even once, and she hadn't felt as if she had to explain why she couldn't do as well as her sisters had. The teachers here didn't even know her sisters.

Reluctantly, though, she walked to the first of the three-times-a-week sessions she'd have with Dr. Hampton, the camp's psychologist and counselor. There was nothing she needed to talk about, nothing she wanted to say, and she dreaded Dr.

Hampton's deep, steady gaze.

Dr. Hampton's office was clean and spare, like a house someone had just moved into. Two testimonials and three framed diplomas hung on one of the walls, which were tinted a pale, restful blue. There was a nearly bare desk at one side of the room, but under the windows was a grouping of two chairs and a sofa, upholstered in a cheerful floral pattern, a low glass coffee table separating them. On the table was a bowl of wild pink summer roses mingled with white sprays of baby's breath.

"Sit down, Emily," Dr. Hampton said with a smile. "Would you like a soft drink? A glass of water?"

"A Coke, please," Emily answered, and a frosty can of Coke appeared as if by magic.

Dr. Hampton sat on the sofa, across from Emily. The sun through the window backlit her hair, causing the red to glow. *She almost looks pretty,* Emily thought.

"Emily," Dr. Hampton said, "how often have you been bribed by your parents to work harder on your studies?"

Emily blinked with surprise. "Bribed?"

"Yes, bribed. Offered rewards for grades. You know, five dollars for each A, season baseball tickets for a perfect report card. Or maybe lunch and a movie."

Emily felt her cheeks grow hot and looked down, embarrassed that she was blushing. "They called them rewards, not bribery."

"Rewards come as a happy surprise after the fact. Bribery involves promised rewards if something is accomplished." Dr. Hampton didn't wait for Emily to answer her original question but went on. "We — the staff at the Foxworth-Isaacson Educational Center — want to treat the cause, not the effect, of underachievement. We feel that a student's low expectations of self are the root of the problem.

"You are a bright girl, Emily, with no reason not to excel in your studies. So let's try to find out what has caused you to believe that you can't succeed."

"I *don't* believe I can't succeed," Emily said, unable to keep a tone of resentment from sliding into her words. Why couldn't people just leave her alone? "My grades are okay."

"Okay? Are you willing to settle for less than the best?"

"I do my homework. I study."

"Granted. But the reports your parents received from your teachers mention that you avoid participating in class discussions, that you cling to seats in the back rows, that you try not to make eye contact with your teachers. Why is that, Emily?"

"Look, there are plenty of kids who like all the attention. I just don't happen to be one of them."

"Would your older sisters have anything to do with this feeling on your part?"

Here we go again, Emily thought. It wasn't the first time a well-meaning teacher had brought up her award-winning sisters. "I'm proud of Angela and Monica," she said, "and I'm not jealous of them. I'm not trying to *be* them. Who they are and what they're doing with their lives have nothing to do with me, and people shouldn't tell me I should be like them when they know good and well I can't be."

Dr. Hampton nodded, as though she were agreeing. "We'll discuss this later," she said. "Would you like to talk about what happened at our group discussion yesterday evening?"

Emily sighed. "Not really," she answered.

"You left when we began talking about our early memories," Dr. Hampton went on, as if Emily had not objected. "Is there something about delving into early memories that disturbs you?"

"Could we talk about something else?" Emily asked. There was a long pause before Dr. Hampton answered, "Of course. If you'd rather. We want you to be comfortable here, Emily."

Emily looked into Dr. Hampton's deep brown eyes and surprised herself by thinking, *I don't believe you. I really don't think you do.*

CHAPTER 8

This camp is a golden opportunity for success and recognition for our entire staff. When the results of our work are made public, there will be praise from educators across the country. I should have that praise. I deserve it. For years I've struggled to achieve it.

I am not about to lose all I've worked for because of Emily Wood.

Is she unable to remember her early childhood experiences? Or does she not want to remember?

At our noon staff meeting, when this was discussed, some felt one way, some the other. I'm the only one who thought it was essential to find out. Of course, I kept my opinion to myself. I'm determined that those memories will never be made public.

I refuse to worry. I keep reminding myself, there is more than one way to blot out a memory.

CHAPTER 9

Emily's group had beach activity scheduled before lunch, but before anyone could get into the water, Coach Jinks began to shout out camp rules through a megaphone. At first Emily tried to pay attention to the list of regulations, wincing at the pitiful jokes with which the coach tried to break up the monotony. But without so much as a wisp of breeze the hot sun toasted Emily's bare shoulders and back, and she was eager to plunge into the chill of the lake.

"So that's what the mama fish said to the baby fish," Coach finished, and waited for laughter. It didn't come.

Embarrassed for him, Emily thought eagerly about the small dock and rowboat she had discovered. The path would be shaded, the water would be sun-dappled and cool, and she'd be away from Coach and his awful jokes and rules in which she wasn't the least bit interested. She edged away from the open beach and back toward the buildings.

Intent on explaining procedure during relay races, Coach didn't seem to notice as she left. Neither did the others on the beach. Within a few minutes Emily had slipped out of their sight, found the almost hidden path, and followed it.

It didn't take long to reach the lake. Faintly, in the distance, she could hear Coach's insistent voice through the megaphone, but the silence captured by the snug glen wrapped around her like a soft blanket. At the end of the dock the rowboat bobbed lightly over waves that lapped the rocks, and far across the water a bird skimmed the surface, then soared out of sight.

Emily stepped onto the dock, which creaked and rocked a little under her weight — but she stopped as she spotted a hand-printed sign posted on a nearby tree: KEEP OFF.

The sign hadn't been there the day before. Emily knew she would have seen and remembered it. Who had put it there? And why? The dock seemed sturdy enough, and Emily was sick of rules. Deliberately, she walked onto the dock and stood at the end, curling her bare toes around the sanded plank as she stared down into the dark blue water.

Behind her the dock groaned, and it rolled under her feet. Emily whirled around, startled.

"Hey, this place you found — it's cool," Taylor said. Dressed like Emily in a two-piece swimsuit, she stood at the foot of the dock, a pleased smile on her face.

Trying not to treat Taylor as an intruder, Emily searched for the right thing to say, but before she could say anything, Taylor shrugged and explained, "I followed you. Okay?"

Emily nodded. "I got tired of listening to all those rules."

"Me too." Taylor walked gingerly until she was at Emily's side. "The dock rocks," she said, then giggled.

"It's old," Emily said, "but I don't think there's any problem with it."

Taylor twisted to glance toward the sign. "That says to keep off."

"It doesn't mean us," Emily said. "The dock seems safe enough. I think they just don't want a whole bunch of kids on it at the same time."

Taylor leaned over to examine the water. "It's deep down there," she said, "and there are a lot of rocks. Do you think there are snakes?"

"Not near the camp," Emily said. "My

dad told me once that cottonmouths try to avoid people."

"Good," Taylor said. "I like to swim, but not with snakes." Emily noticed that Taylor's pale skin was already glowing pink.

"Didn't you put on sunblock?" Emily asked.

"I didn't bring any," Taylor said. She quickly straightened and turned to face Emily, defensive.

"I've got some sunblock in my room that hardly anybody else uses except doctors and their families," Emily said quickly. "You can have some. You haven't been out in the sun much. You're going to get a bad burn if you don't use anything."

Taylor began to look interested. "How come hardly anybody uses it?"

"Because it's a total block and terribly expensive," Emily answered.

Taylor smiled. "Well, okay, then," she said. "Lead me to it."

A few minutes later, as Emily finished rubbing sunblock into Taylor's back and shoulders, Taylor said, "I don't care if some people say I look weird. I like to be different. Does it bother you?"

"No," Emily said. "I think you should look any way you want to look."

"Any way?"

"Sure," Emily said. "Whatever makes you happy." She thought about her older sisters and her parents' disappointment that she wasn't just like them. "People can't be carbon copies of other people," she said.

"Unless they want to be," Taylor added.

Emily nodded and tried not to smile as she momentarily wondered what her parents would think if she came home with spiked pink-and-gold hair.

"Do you think the coach is finally through explaining all his rules and will let us go swimming now?" Taylor asked.

"Let's find out," Emily said. She threw open the bedroom door. "Race you!"

After a swim, beach volleyball, a shower, and lunch, Emily found herself captured by Haley and steered toward one of Camp Excel's waiting vans. "I found the name and address of a *curandero*," Haley said in a low voice, excitedly digging her fingers into Emily's arm.

"Ouch," Emily said, and tried to pull away.

"You could at least say thank you." Haley shoved Emily into the backseat and squeezed in beside her.

"Okay, then, thank you," Emily said. "How did you find him?"

"Computer room, Internet," Haley said. "No problem. Did you bring any money?"

"Of course," Emily told her. "It's a sight-seeing and shopping trip, isn't it?" She thought a moment, then confronted Haley. "How much is visiting this so-called folk healer going to cost?"

Haley looked pained. "Don't be like that, Em. He's a true healer. He doesn't charge."

Emily leaned back against the seat, relieved.

"He simply asks for donations," Haley said. Quickly, she added, "Like a few dollars. I mean whatever you think his advice is worth. And he sells his special charms and candles. You understand he has to charge for those just to break even."

Emily sighed and squeezed over even farther as at least a dozen Camp Excel campers climbed into the van. Taylor, getting into the front seat, smiled at Emily and waved.

Emily smiled back. "Why don't we just visit antique shops or the local pizza place?" she asked Haley.

Haley fixed Emily with a firm gaze. "And take chances with your future? Absolutely not. I feel responsible for you because I introduced you to the runes in the first place. We're going to keep the appointment I made with the *curandero*."

★ ★ ★

Lampley's picturesque brick courthouse and steeple towered over a square pocket park, complete with gazebo and historical marker. Facing the streets that surrounded it on three sides were wood-front shops that looked as if they came out of a small Western movie set. There was even a narrow, windowless building with a sign over the doorway: LAMPLEY HISTORICAL MUSEUM.

"We'll meet back here in two hours. Don't be late!" their driver cautioned.

The passengers scattered in every direction. "See you," Taylor called to Emily as she jaywalked across the nearly empty street.

Haley hustled Emily halfway down the block before she stopped, pulled a scrap of paper from the pocket of her shorts, and studied it. "We have to find South A Street," she said.

Emily looked back. "Why don't we ask our driver?"

"No." Haley frowned at Emily. "We're not going to tell anyone about the *curandero*, and we're absolutely not going to tell them what advice he gives."

"No one will know? Good. Then they won't think we're crazy," Emily said.

"That's not why we can't tell." Haley rolled her eyes and threw a look of impatience at Emily. "We can't tell because we don't know where the evil directed at you is coming from. We have to keep secret the help the *curandero* will give you. Understand?"

Emily nodded, not wanting another lecture.

"Promise you won't tell?" Haley persisted.

"Promise," Emily said, wishing she hadn't given in to Haley so easily. The runes were silly, but the *curandero* was a person, and Emily was both embarrassed at what he might think and afraid of what he might tell her.

It took Haley only a minute to get directions from a salesperson in the nearest shop. "It's just one street over and down a few blocks," Haley repeated to Emily.

The picturesque part of Lampley vanished at the end of South A Street, where the pavement deteriorated into a rutted dirt road. Dust flew up with each step, and two small, yapping terriers, roaming free, sniffed at the girls' heels until they seemed satisfied that they meant no harm. White painted clapboard houses decorated with big porches and boxes overflowing with red geraniums became small homes with cluttered open carports and an occasional rusting car without wheels resting on cement blocks.

Emily was nervous about going too much farther out of town, but Haley finally stopped in front of a house with a chain-link fence. On it was a sign: YERBERIA.

"That means herb shop," Haley explained happily. "This is the place." She opened the gate and walked to the broken front step, reaching up to ring the doorbell. Emily followed.

The door was opened by a man wearing a spotless white shirt and trousers, a gold cross on a chain hanging halfway down his chest. "Good afternoon," he said. "I am Alberto Salgado."

"The *curandero?*" Haley asked.

"*Sí,* I am a *curandero,*" he said. "Are you Miss Haley Griffin?"

"*Sí* — uh — yes," Haley said. "And this is Emily Wood, the one I told you about."

"Please come into my shop," Mr. Salgado said. He stepped aside, holding the door wide.

The dimly lit room smelled like fried onions and incense. Over the hum of a window air conditioner, a baby's sleepy cries could be heard, and there were the clattering sounds of pans and dishes coming from what must be a kitchen.

Two sides of the room were occupied by low cabinets on which were arrayed statues of saints, candles, and bottles that contained strange dark liquids. On a small table lay an assortment of charms and pendants beside a card on which was hand-printed, $15 APIECE.

The walls were covered with crucifixes of all sizes and framed prints of religious paintings. Rosaries hung from pegs on each side of a doorway leading into a hall. Facing the windows, in the middle of the center wall, stood what looked like a makeshift altar with statues and candles in glass holders placed on a lace-trimmed white cloth.

In front of the altar sat an overstuffed chair, the top, back, and armrests covered with huge crocheted doilies. Opposite the chair was a matching sofa, its original hues faded into a colorless smear.

Mr. Salgado motioned to the sofa, and Haley immediately sat down, pulling Emily with her.

As Mr. Salgado seated himself opposite them, Haley said, "Em has received two warnings from Loki, which she has drawn from the runes. She must be in danger, but we don't know what it is or where it's coming from."

Mr. Salgado pursed his lips and shook his head. "I am not familiar with Loki or the runes."

"You don't know about Loki?"

"I follow my own path," he explained, "Or, should I say, my father's path, for he was a *curandero* before me. I give consultations and advise people on how to cure their illnesses or solve their problems. Occasionally, when it is necessary, I will go beyond giving advice in order to perform a purification rite."

Emily squirmed to the edge of her seat. "Maybe we should —"

Haley leaned forward, ignoring her. "We know that Em is in danger. Will your way tell us what we can do about it?"

Mr. Salgado nodded. "If it is in my power," he said. Before Haley could answer, he added, "I am considered a very successful *curandero*. In the winter, when I reside down in the valley, I sometimes receive as many as fifty clients a day."

Emily attempted to stand. "I think we ought to —"

Haley grabbed her wrist, pulling her down. "Tell us what we should do," she said to Mr. Salgado.

As he walked to the windows, lowering the shades to darken the room, Haley hissed at Emily, "Sit still, and keep quiet. This is for your own good."

Mr. Salgado seated himself again, and Emily was surprised to see that he had wrapped a white robe over his clothing.

Although the light in the room was dim, Mr. Salgado reached out and took both of Emily's hands in his. He bent his head over her open palms, studying them.

After a moment he raised his head, his face close to her own. "You are in good health," he told her. "I can feel a vital energy passing through your body. The danger your friend spoke of does not come from any physical condition."

Releasing her hands, he stood and lit the candles on the altar behind his chair. A spiral of smoke rose from the small incense bowl, and Emily wrinkled her nose at its oversweet aroma.

Mr. Salgado reached down to the floor next to his chair and picked up a lapboard. Next, he pulled an old, stained deck of ornate picture cards from a pocket in his robe and began to lay them out on the board.

"Tarot?" Haley asked as she leaned close to watch.

"No," Mr. Salgado said. "I told you, I follow my own path."

For a long moment Emily watched as Mr. Salgado swept up the cards, shuffled them, then laid them out again. During this time the room was silent except for low, murmuring whispers that occasionally escaped his lips.

When he finally drew the cards together and looked directly into Emily's eyes, she leaned as far back against the sofa as she could and shivered. "What are you going to tell me?" she asked, dreading his answer.

"Your friend is right," he said. "You are in danger."

"How?" Emily asked. "Danger from what?"

"There is something locked inside you," Mr. Salgado said. "As long as it is within you, you are in danger."

"You said she was healthy," Haley complained.

"The hidden thing is not something of the body. It is something of the mind."

"What is it?" Emily asked, frightened in spite of her resolve not to believe.

"I do not know," he said. "I see a death. Perhaps a second one."

Emily shivered as cold gripped her neck and shoulders. She heard Haley gasp. "*My* death?" Emily whispered.

"I do not know," Mr. Salgado answered.

"All I can tell you is that the only way to counter this danger is to find what is locked inside you and rid yourself of it. No one can do this for you. You must do it yourself."

"But if I don't know what it is —"

"I think you know."

"I don't! Honestly!"

"Then you must search."

"How?"

"I explained, I can't tell you that. But I can give you a potion of special oils designed to ward off evil. Keep it on your person." As if by magic, a small, clear plastic vial with a cork stopper appeared in Mr. Salgado's right hand. Inside the three-inch tube Emily could see a dark sludge. As she took the vial from him, the substance swirled heavily and slowly like a thick oil.

"How will this help me?" she whispered.

"I cannot tell you that. I can only assure you that you'll know when the time comes. In the meantime the potion will protect you."

"Is that all you can say?" Emily demanded. "I need to know what to do."

Haley rested a hand on Emily's arm. "Keep the potion in your pocket," she told her, again in charge. "We'll meditate. Together we'll search. We'll find out what's locked inside you."

Emily stared from Mr. Salgado to Haley to the dark tube in her hands, suddenly astonished that for a few moments she had actually believed all this hocus-pocus about danger and protective potions . . . because of the nightmares, because of the runes . . . yet none of it made sense. Sitting here in this strange room was probably one of the craziest things she had ever done in her life.

Mr. Salgado held out a wide clay bowl. Inside it lay two crumpled twenty-dollar bills. "The potion costs ten dollars," he said. "There is no charge for the reading. I ask only for a goodwill donation in addition."

Emily held the potion out to him. "I really don't need —" she began.

Haley snatched the vial and tucked it firmly into the pocket of Emily's polo shirt. "You do need it!" she said.

Emily sighed. She pulled her wallet out of her small handbag, pulled out a twenty-dollar bill, and laid it on top of the others in the bowl.

"Thank you," Mr. Salgado said. He laid the bowl on the altar and snuffed out the candles.

As he stood he frowned at Emily, who looked away, puzzled. Had he expected her to pay more? Well, she wouldn't. She was sorry she'd been intimidated into parting with twenty dollars.

Haley bought a few things, but Emily wasn't interested enough to pay attention to what they were. She shouldn't have been here. She shouldn't have allowed Haley to bring her.

"Miss Wood," Mr. Salgado said as he opened the front door, "you are resentful that your friend brought you here and angry that I have not told you more about what you should do to ward off the evil that is set against you. Yet at the same time you do not believe that what I have told you is true."

"I — I'm sorry," Emily said. "I just think that if I really am in some kind of danger, you should tell me more about what to expect." She shook her head, trying to get rid of the thoughts that were confusing her. "What I really mean is that I don't believe in Loki and runes and evil and all that. I am not hiding anything —"

She stopped abruptly. *But maybe I am,* she thought. *If I were really truthful I'd admit that I couldn't be sure.*

CHAPTER 10

Emily went to the dock again, paying no attention to the sign I posted to absolve the camp of any blame.

The peaceful water, the rocks, the silence of this solitary spot . . . they've tempted her. I was sure she would return. I'm equally positive she'll return again.

CHAPTER 11

"Promise me!" Haley repeated as they arrived back at the town square with less than ten minutes to spare before pickup time. "You must keep the potion with you at all times!"

"Why do you keep insisting?" Emily asked.

"Because I feel responsible for you. If a car were speeding toward you, I'd push you out of the way, wouldn't I? If I saw you going under out in the lake, I'd rescue you. Well, this is the same thing. I've discovered you are in danger, and even proved it to you through Mr. Salgado. So now I have to make sure you're protected from the danger, whether I want to or not."

Emily gave Haley a sharp look. "Okay, I'll make a bargain with you."

"What kind of a bargain?"

Emily held up her right hand. "I'll keep the potion with me at all times if you agree not to make me draw one of the runes each morning."

Haley grimaced but answered, "Well, okay, I guess. We don't know how much longer this period of danger will last, and I know I'd get absolutely sick to my stomach if you picked Loki again. I might die on the spot."

"You wouldn't die," Emily retorted.

"That's right. I wouldn't. I'd just feel like it," Haley said. "It's bad enough having to feel responsible for you. Everyone in my family is always after me: 'Be responsible about cleaning your room.' 'Be responsible about doing your homework.' 'Be responsible, be responsible.' I hate being responsible."

"Then let's forget all about Mr. Salgado and what he told us."

"No. We can't. And you'll thank me later, especially after we begin meditating."

"Now what are you talking about?"

"Meditating. Mr. Salgado said the answer is hidden within you, so we have to reach inside your mind and find out what is causing the problem."

"It's not going to work."

"We at least have to try."

"If we try it once, will you stop bugging — ?" Emily began. She broke off as Haley's eyes suddenly widened and her mouth dropped open. "What's the matter with you?"

103

Since Haley seemed unable to answer, Emily twisted around to see what she was staring at. She felt her own mouth open with surprise.

Leaving a beauty parlor across the street was a girl with white-blond, curly hair fanning out around her face.

Emily gasped. "Who is that?"

"Someone trying to be you." Haley groaned and said, "It's pink-and-gold Taylor. Only she's not pink and gold anymore."

Silently Emily and Haley watched Taylor approach. As Taylor came near she grinned happily. Her face was clean of all makeup.

"Surprise!" she said. "Don't you love it?"

Still in shock, Emily murmured, "You — uh — look like — like —"

"You!" Taylor said. She was obviously so delighted that Emily was reminded of a little kid at a birthday party.

"Why?" Haley asked.

"I like the way Emily's hair looks."

"But what about your one-of-a-kind look?" Haley asked.

"This will be one-of-a-kind when I get home," Taylor said. "Nobody in my hometown has ever seen Emily." She happily fingered a curly twist of hair. "It's cool," she said. "I picked out a shade as close to your

hair color as I could get, and they s.
me how to make it look like this wi.
curling iron. Now I can let it fall in front ͺ
my face and hide behind it, just like you
do."

"Why try to look like Emily? Why not just
be yourself?" Haley rolled her eyes again.

Taylor threw Haley an exasperated
glance. "Come off it, Haley," she said. "I'm
not trying to look like Emily. Only the hair."
She touched her face with her fingertips and
giggled. "I feel naked without any makeup.
The stylist creamed it off. She said it didn't
go with the light hair. I'll try to find something else that will work. Maybe rose or light
green eye shadow?"

Haley didn't answer, so Taylor turned to
Emily. "Are you mad at me, too?" she
asked.

Emily softened at the open hurt on Taylor's face. "I'm not mad at you," she answered. "I'm just surprised. The change
you've made takes getting used to." She
kept her gaze on Taylor as she said, "For the
first time I can see what you really look like.
You're pretty, Taylor. Your cheekbones are
high, like a model's. I hadn't noticed
before."

"Then you don't care that I copied your
hair?"

"I don't care," Emily said, although she wasn't really sure how she felt. It was strange seeing a reflection of herself in another person. No one had ever seemed to think she was worth copying before.

She glanced up to see some of the other kids from their van arriving. A few stared from Emily to Taylor and back again. One of the girls gasped, turning around too late to hide the startled expression on her face.

Emily slumped, letting her hair fall forward, hiding behind it. She should have realized immediately that what Taylor had done would attract attention. She hated being stared at. She hated being noticed. She wished with all her power that Taylor hadn't chosen to imitate her.

The van drove up and the driver jumped out, throwing the side doors open. Emily climbed into the van, choosing a seat in the back, as far from everyone else as she could get.

Wishing she were invisible, Emily didn't speak during the drive back to Camp Excel. The others didn't seem to care. They were all busy talking. Emily heard scraps of conversation about some of the shops in Lampley, about its funny little museum, and once she caught Taylor's name and her own. As someone giggled, Emily cringed and slid even farther down in the seat.

When the van pulled up to the parking area in front of the central building, Emily, head down, followed everyone out. She started toward the main building but was stopped when Haley grasped her arm.

"Where are you going?" Haley asked.

Emily pulled her arm away and looked at her watch. "I've got an appointment with Dr. Anderson at five-thirty. I don't want to be late."

Haley gave an impatient shrug. "Oh, that. Big nothing. Because Dr. Lorene Anderson's the chief assistant to Dr. Isaacson, she writes his student reports. I met with her this morning. She'll just ask you a bunch of questions about stuff you're interested in and if you've set any goals for yourself. You know. You've heard it all before. It won't take long. I'll wait for you."

Across the way Emily saw Taylor enter the dorm. She thought ahead to when they'd both show up for dinner and knew how people would stare and talk. She couldn't bear it. She'd skip dinner. She'd send word that she wasn't hungry and stay in her room.

"Em?" Haley asked. "Aren't you listening? I said I'd wait for you. We can stick around a few minutes, then go in to dinner together."

"No," Emily said. "Don't wait. I don't want you to wait." She ran from Haley into the cool, air-conditioned building, shivering at the sudden drop in temperature.

The lobby was empty, so she relaxed a little, standing still, closing her eyes, and taking three deep breaths. For a moment she knew she'd been close to panic, and panic wouldn't help any situation.

What difference would it make if people stared? she asked herself. *It shouldn't really matter to me what people think.*

But hadn't she always felt afraid to be noticed, to be the focus of staring eyes? Wasn't she more secure in back rows and quiet corners, hidden behind her curtain of hair?

Why have I always been like this? Emily wondered. She ached to know the answer, but there was none.

Slowly she walked down the hallway. There were names on a few of the doors. She passed Dr. Lydia Hampton's office and, across the hall, the office and clinic run by Maria Jimenez, the nurse.

The next door was about twenty-five feet farther down the hall, and it stood ajar. Dr. Kendrick Isaacson's name was on the door and, as she approached, Emily couldn't help glancing inside. The floor was covered in the same neutral wall-to-wall carpeting as in the rest of the building, but the mahogany desk against the far wall was immense, with deep carvings on either side. A burgundy-red leather chair sat at an angle behind the desk. No one was in sight, so out of curiosity Emily took a cautious step inside the room. On the left side of the large room was a credenza on which a massive bowl of fresh flowers rested. A small tapestry hung above it.

At the far right of the room was a grouping of comfortable chairs around a low table. Behind the table were two large framed portraits. One was of Dr. Isaacson, and the other . . .

Emily stared at the second portrait, frozen, feeling the blood drain from her face. She reached out blindly, trying to grasp something — anything — to steady herself. Unable to breathe, she gulped frantically for air. The woman . . . the smiling woman in the portrait . . . it was the same face that over and over and over again thrust itself into Emily's nightmares. Glassy eyes in a photograph . . . eyes in a dead, bloody face . . . same eyes . . . same person.

Darkness smothered Emily's vision and swirled into her mind. She felt herself falling.

★ ★ ★

Emily awoke to find herself on a cot in a white, sterile-looking room. She struggled to sit up, but Mrs. Jimenez stepped into her vision. Her firm hand pushed Emily back onto the cot, and she said, "You're in my clinic, sweetie. You passed out. How are you feeling now?"

Emily took a deep breath. "Okay," she said.

Mrs. Jimenez took Emily's pulse and said, "Everything checks out. No temperature. You haven't got a sore throat, have you? Sick to your stomach? Anything like that?"

"No," Emily said.

"Ever fainted before?"

"No."

"Is it that time of the month?"

"No."

"Your color's good. Here. I'll give you a hand. Let's see if you can sit up."

Emily swung her legs over the edge of the cot as Mrs. Jimenez helped her to a sitting position.

"Dizzy?" Mrs. Jimenez asked.

"No."

Mrs. Jimenez pursed her lips as she thought, then asked, "When did you last eat?"

"At lunchtime," Emily answered.

"And probably not much at that," Mrs. Jimenez said. "You girls are always either eating junk food or dieting. Well, stay here a few minutes. Dr. Anderson wants to talk to you."

"Oh!" Emily said. She looked at her watch. Fifteen minutes to six. She could imagine the looks of disappointment on her parents' faces that she'd been at camp only a day and had already blown it. "I'm late for my appointment."

To her surprise, Mrs. Jimenez smiled. "Don't worry about it. If you can't go to Dr. Anderson, she'll come to you. Stay here. I'll go get her."

Emily leaned back against the wall, closing her eyes, seeing once again the portrait of the woman on the wall in Dr. Isaacson's office. Who was she? And why did she keep showing up in Emily's dreams?

"Are you asleep?"

Emily's eyelids flew open, and she struggled to sit upright. Still concerned, she said, "Dr. Anderson, I'm sorry that I didn't keep my appointment on time."

"There's no need to apologize," Dr. Anderson told her. "What happened was beyond your control." She smiled as she pulled up a white metal chair to sit facing Emily.

Even in her staff uniform Dr. Anderson was attractive, Emily thought. Her brown hair was short enough to curl around her cheeks, and at the moment her green eyes looked warm and sympathetic. She was probably about the same height as Emily, and every bit as slender, even though she had to be close to fifty.

"Do you know why you fainted?" Dr. Anderson asked.

I can't tell you. I can't tell anyone, Emily thought. Trying to sidestep the question, she said, "The door to Dr. Isaacson's office was standing open. I was curious. I stepped inside to take a good look."

"Did you like what you saw?"

"Yes. It all looks important, the way I suppose the office of the director of an educational center should look." Emily cleared her throat before she added, "That's an impressive photograph of Dr. Isaacson on the wall over the chairs."

Dr. Anderson gave a brief nod and another smile but didn't speak.

Again Emily cleared her throat. "The other picture — who is the woman?"

"Dr. Amelia Foxworth," Dr. Anderson said. "She and Dr. Isaacson were partners. They founded the educational center together." She smiled as she added, "With the help of a handpicked staff, of course. Myself, Dr. Hampton, Dr. Bonaduce, Mrs. —"

"Where is Dr. Foxworth?" Emily interrupted.

"She's no longer with us," Dr. Anderson said.

"Do you mean she moved away?"

"No. She died."

Emily steeled herself to ask the next question. "How?"

Dr. Anderson hesitated a moment, studying Emily. Then she answered, "Dr. Foxworth died in a fall."

Emily's head began to hurt. "When?" she managed to ask.

"About seven . . . no, eight years ago, I think. Why do you ask?"

"I — I just wondered," Emily said. As she leaned back against the wall she closed her eyes and shivered. The face in her nightmare had imprinted itself on her brain.

Moist leaves and curling tendrils of honeysuckle vines plastered her face as she poked her head from the tunnel of green. Ahead of her, at eye level, lay bright blue water and gleaming tiles, but in the background two discordant voices thrummed high and low, shrill and angry, like string instruments being tuned before a symphony.

Suddenly a body slammed to the tile of the pool, half in, half out of the water, eyes staring, holding Emily's gaze as though she were hypnotized. A blinding flash of light broke the spell, and Emily squirmed back into the tunnel. She could hear a frantic, demanding voice calling from far away: "You! Little girl! Don't leave! Come back here!"

Then something else. What was the voice saying?

The green tunnel threatened to smother Emily as she clawed her way back through the branches and tangles. And the voice . . .

"Emily?" she heard Dr. Anderson saying. "I asked if you knew why you fainted. Can you tell me?"

Emily opened her eyes. Dr. Anderson was studying her with concern. In the doorway Mrs. Jimenez also looked on. Emily remembered what Mrs. Jimenez had said. "I guess I was hungry," she answered.

"See? What did I tell you?" Mrs. Jimenez spoke up. "Dieting. These girls are always dieting. They don't eat enough to keep a bird alive because they want to be skinny. Then they get a cheeseburger with double fries and don't count it because they also order a Diet Coke."

Dr. Anderson didn't respond to Mrs. Jimenez's excited tirade. She didn't take her

114

eyes off Emily's face. Finally she stood and said, "It's about time for our regular staff meeting. If you need me, Emily, if you have any problems you want to talk over, just let me know. I'm here for you."

"Thank you," Emily said, relieved that there would be no more questions — at least for now.

Dr. Anderson left, and Mrs. Jimenez stepped forward. "The dinner bell is going to ring in just a couple of minutes. Some food will be good for you. Do you feel up to walking into the dining room?"

"No, I don't," Emily said quickly, leaping at this chance to avoid Taylor and the others. "I'm still kind of shaky."

"Then I'll call for a tray to be sent here," Mrs. Jimenez said. "Just lie down until it arrives and take it easy. I'll shut the door and let you rest."

Emily did as she was told. Through the closed door she heard Mrs. Jimenez's voice on the phone in her office, a soft up-and-down buzz like a fly against a window screen. The cotton blanket on the cot was soft and soothing as Emily pulled it up to her chin. Mercifully, the face in her mind had left, and suddenly she was very tired. As she rolled onto her side, curling her knees to her chin, she decided to do as Mrs. Jimenez had suggested and rest, if only for a minute. Within seconds she was asleep.

She opened her eyes to a darkened room with only a night-light gleaming at the base of one wall.

"Well, it's about time," Haley said from the chair where Dr. Anderson had been sitting earlier. She stood up and flipped on the overhead light. "When you didn't come in to dinner, I went looking for you. Mrs. Jimenez said you fainted because you hadn't been eating enough."

Emily didn't say anything. If that excuse seemed to satisfy everyone, she'd let it ride.

"Have you got your potion with you?"

Emily touched the pocket of her shirt and felt the small vial still in place. "Yes," she said. Sitting up, she swung her feet to the floor. "What did everyone say about Taylor's hair?" she asked.

"Taylor didn't show at dinner, either," Haley said. "I think she wanted to make a dramatic entrance with you. Maybe she went looking for you, too."

Swept by guilt, Emily said, "I wish she hadn't picked me to imitate. At first I didn't mind, but when everyone —"

The loud wail of a siren drowned out the rest of her words. As it went into a continuing short burst pattern, Emily asked, "Fire drill?"

"No one warned us about a drill. Maybe it's the real thing," Haley shouted over the noise. "Let's get out of here."

There was no sign of fire or stench of smoke as they stepped into the hall and strode quickly toward the main door of the building.

Emily pushed it open as one of the other campers rushed past.

Another, coming up from the lake area, grabbed the camper's arm and cried out, "It's that girl with all the white hair — Emily! Somebody found her in the water. I think she drowned."

CHAPTER 12

It had to happen.

Ending her life was an unpleasant task, but it couldn't be avoided. I suppose most of the staff believed that story that Emily Wood fainted because she hadn't been eating, but I know better. She fainted because she recognized Dr. Foxworth in the portrait. She remembered. She knew. And before long she would have told.

But now there is no more need to worry. It's over.

CHAPTER 13

Haley stared at Emily, her eyes wide with horror. "Taylor?" she whispered.

Emily didn't answer. Dizzy and sick with guilt and fear, she raced toward a cluster of people who were staring down at the ground. Of course it was Taylor. It had to be Taylor. Why hadn't she objected when Taylor tried to copy her? Why hadn't she warned Taylor about Loki and the danger?

What am I thinking? Shocked by her thoughts, Emily told herself, *There is no Loki. There are no magic stones. What happened to Taylor can't be my fault!*

As she reached the circle of onlookers, Emily frantically shoved two of them aside and burst into the inner ring.

"Hey! Watch where you're going!" someone complained, but Emily ignored him.

Taylor, her clothes soaking wet, her hair hanging in sopping strings, sat on the ground. Mrs. Jimenez sat with her, her left arm supporting Taylor. With her right hand and a thick pad of bloodstained cloth, she applied pressure to a gash at the back of Taylor's head.

"Move along, everybody. Stay out of the way," Coach Jinks kept saying, but no one paid attention to him.

Taylor hadn't drowned! She was alive! Everything began to come back into focus for Emily, who stood still, sucking in deep breaths, willing herself to calm down. She became aware that Dr. Isaacson stood nearby with Dr. Weil and Mrs. Comstock, matching frowns of concern on their faces as they watched Mrs. Jimenez administering aid to Taylor. Oddly, Dr. Isaacson's right arm rested on Maxwell's shoulders, but Emily didn't try to figure out why. All that mattered was that Taylor would be all right.

The fire alarm stopped abruptly, the sudden silence jarring. Then from the far distance came the wail of sirens.

Emily dropped to her knees beside Taylor. "How badly is she hurt?" she asked Mrs. Jimenez.

"She may need a couple of stitches," Mrs. Jimenez said. She glanced in the direction of the road to the camp. "But she's not going to need the pumper and ambulance they're sending. That's for sure."

"Pulling the fire alarm was the best way I knew of to get help in a hurry," Maxwell said.

Mrs. Jimenez looked up. "You're smart," she said. "You did the right thing."

Maxwell dropped to his haunches next to Emily, peering at her from under the rolled edge of his cap. Lowering his voice, he said, "I thought she was you."

Taylor reached out and took Emily's hand, clutching it tightly. "I wanted to go in to dinner with you," she said, "but I couldn't find you anywhere. Then I remembered the quiet place you went when I followed you yesterday. Down at the lake. That little dock. I thought you might have gone there again."

Through the tangle of vines and trees, Emily thought. "At the little dock," she repeated.

Taylor was silent, so Emily asked, "Then what happened?"

"Nothing," Taylor answered.

"Something must have happened to you. Did you trip? Did you lose your balance? How did you get hurt?"

"I don't know," Taylor said. "You weren't there. No one was there. The sun was going down, so I walked out on the dock to watch. There was just a thin line of yellow and green and blue in the sky along the water toward the west. Even the row-boat that was tied to the dock looked kind of silvery in the light. A bird suddenly swooped down toward the water. I stepped back, and the dock shook a little bit. That's all I remember."

Mrs. Jimenez bent to look down into Taylor's face. "You were on that little dock where it says 'keep out'?"

"Yes."

"Don't you believe in signs?"

"How did you know about the dock?" Emily asked.

"I manage to get around," Mrs. Jimenez said. "You think the staff doesn't know what's going on? We all do."

"Then tell me, please," Emily said. "What happened to Taylor?"

Mrs. Jimenez said, "Only one thing could have happened. Taylor slipped and fell and hit her head. Luckily somebody came along to pull her out of the water."

"Maxwell?" Emily turned toward him. "Was it you? Were you with Taylor? You said you thought Taylor was me."

"I saw you — uh, her — disappear down the trail, and I followed," Maxwell said. "I wanted to talk to you."

"Then you saw Taylor fall?"

Maxwell shook his head. "I wasn't that close to her, and it was getting dark. I heard a kind of thunk and a splash, but when I got close to the dock no one was in sight. I thought I heard someone in a rowboat — the splash of oars, I mean — so I went to the end of the dock and there I could barely see your — no, I mean Taylor's — white hair all spread out and wavy under the surface of the water like seaweed. So I reached down and tugged her out. She coughed up some water and was breathing all right, but her head was bleeding, so I carried her up here, dumped her on the grass, and pulled the fire alarm to get help."

The sirens on the vehicles whined to a stop as they reached Camp Excel, and soon three men in volunteers' uniforms came running. "Back, step back," one of them shouted, and Emily pulled her hand from Taylor's and scrambled out of the way.

A few seconds later one of the volunteers on his knees beside Taylor said, "A doc should probably see to that cut on her head. Lampley doesn't have an emergency hospital, so we'll take her into Marble Falls."

"I'll go with her," Mrs. Jimenez told him.

"I'll go, too," Emily said.

"No." Dr. Isaacson stepped forward and clamped a firm hand on Emily's shoulder.

"Thank you for your generous offer, Emily," he said, "but it would be more appropriate for you to remain at camp. Mrs. Jimenez's presence should be sufficient."

Emily kept her eyes on Taylor's bedraggled, bloody hair. "I just thought Taylor would feel better if someone she knew —"

"Mrs. Jimenez will be with her." Abruptly he turned to Coach Jinks and said, "You won't be needed for the session on study skills, so will you please drive one of the Camp Excel vans to the hospital and bring Mrs. Jimenez and Taylor back to camp as soon as Taylor is released?"

As the ambulance and fire truck drove off, the crowd of teachers and kids melted away in small groups. Emily realized that Maxwell and Haley were the only ones who had stayed. "Taylor would have died if you hadn't been there," she said to Maxwell.

Maxwell's sudden look of pleasure turned to embarrassment. "I just did what needed to be done," he said.

Haley nodded agreement. "Sometimes decisions are made for us by forces beyond our control," she said. "You were destined to save Taylor whether you were trying to be a hero or not."

Maxwell groaned. "I wasn't trying to be a hero."

Haley sighed. "Don't fight the forces of fate." She said to Emily, "I'm going to study hall. Are you coming?"

"Later," Emily told her. "First I want to talk to Maxwell."

Haley persisted. "You aren't planning to wander off by yourself and make me worry about you, are you?"

"You don't need to worry about me," Emily answered. "I'll be with Maxwell."

"Have you got — ?"

"It's right here." Emily's fingertips touched the vial in the pocket of her shirt.

As Haley left, walking in the direction of the main building, Maxwell asked Emily, "What do you want to talk about?"

Emily looked at Maxwell intently. Under the yellow globes that lit the path his cheeks and nose were highlighted, but his eyes were nearly hidden by his knit cap.

"Take off your cap," Emily told him.

"What?" Maxwell's hands flew protectively to his head.

"*Please* take off your cap," Emily said. "It hides so much of your face, and I want to know what you really look like."

His gaze never leaving hers, Maxwell slowly removed his cap. His dark hair was plastered to his forehead. His eyes were wide. Without the cap he seemed vulnerable, like a small child.

"Thank you," Emily said. "Now we can talk."

"Not yet," Maxwell told her. From his wrist he pulled one of probably a half-dozen rubber bands and handed it to her.

He didn't need to explain. Emily pulled back her hair, wrapping the rubber band around it to hold it at the nape of her neck. Shyly, feeling as exposed as though she were under a spotlight, she took a deep breath and looked up at Maxwell.

"*Now* we can talk," he said. But looking puzzled, he asked, "What are we going to talk about?"

"First of all," Emily said, "don't be embarrassed by what Haley said. She was right. You really were a hero."

Maxwell's smile grew into a grin. "Maybe I was," he said. He grinned happily. "I may use this whole experience in a play someday. Horton Foote wrote a whole series of plays about his lifetime experiences. I can be just as successful as he was."

"I need you to tell me exactly what happened," Emily said.

"In my play I could bring out the fact that no one in my main character's family could believe he'd ever do anything heroic. His older brother, sure. They'd expect it of him." He looked intently at Emily. "It's okay, you know, to expose your secret family horrors for the stage."

"Maxwell," Emily persisted. "I can't wait until you finally write a play about it to find out what happened to Taylor. Tell me now."

He looked puzzled. "But I did."

Emily tried a different approach. "You gave us the facts but nothing behind them. Tell me everything you saw and heard after you heard the splash and knew that Taylor had fallen into the lake."

"I didn't know it was Taylor. I thought I was following you."

"Okay, me. Go on."

Maxwell's forehead wrinkled as the words tumbled out. "I was scared when I saw Taylor in the water. And Taylor was a dead weight. Maybe it was because I was so scared that I had the strength to pull her out. Adrenaline, you know. I kept hoping that whoever was in the rowboat would come and help, but he was leaving, not coming. Anyhow, when I got Taylor back onto the dock —"

Emily interrupted. "Wait a minute. You said earlier that you heard someone in a rowboat. Now you just said that someone was rowing away. Did you see this person?"

"No. It was too dark and the tree branches that grew out over the water were in the way."

"Taylor told us she saw the rowboat still tied to the dock. She said it looked silvery. Was that rowboat still there at the dock when you got there? Did you hear another rowboat?"

Maxwell scrunched up his face as he thought. "No," he finally said. "I remember clearly. There was no rowboat tied to the dock."

Emily shivered, and her legs wobbled as though they could no longer hold her up. She sat down on the grass, bent over, and pressed her hands to her forehead.

"What's the matter?" Maxwell asked. He perched cross-legged beside her.

Emily sat upright and looked at him intently. "We need to talk about what happened on the dock."

"I told you. Taylor fell into the water, and I —"

"Before that. When you followed her. You said you heard a thunk and a splash."

"That's right."

"When you got to the dock, no one was in sight."

"I said that already."

"I know," Emily told him. "I'm trying to

put it all together. Taylor saw a rowboat. You didn't. You heard a rowboat leaving. Get it?"

Maxwell gave a start of surprise. "You mean someone else was there?"

"Someone had to be there."

"But Taylor didn't see anyone."

Emily shuddered, frightened because she was sure of what must have happened. "Someone was already at the dock when Taylor got there. Or else someone saw Taylor enter the path to the dock and followed her, just as you did. Taylor said the dock shook a little bit. Remember? Probably because someone had stepped onto the dock after her."

Maxwell's eyes opened even wider. "Are you saying that Taylor was hit on the head and knocked into the water?"

"Yes," Emily answered. "I think that's what happened. And then the person who did it heard you coming and couldn't leave by the path or you would have seen him. So he climbed into the rowboat and managed to row out of sight."

"That could have happened," Maxwell said quietly.

"The cut on Taylor's head was at the back. If she'd fallen on the rocks, wouldn't it be more likely that the cut would have been on her forehead?"

"I think so."

For a moment both Emily and Maxwell were silent as they thought about Taylor and what might have happened. Then Maxwell asked, "What I don't understand is, why would anyone want to harm Taylor?"

"I don't think anyone did."

"Then why — ?" Maxwell stared hard at Emily. "Wait a minute. I see what you mean. Taylor looked like you. From a distance I couldn't see her face, so I thought she *was* you. If someone came up behind her and thought she was you . . . but why would someone want to harm *you?*"

"I don't know," Emily said. In a rush she told him about Haley's runes and the Loki stone and the *curandero*. "I know it's hokey, and although Haley believes all that stuff, I don't," Emily said. "But even the *curandero* spoke of danger." She touched the vial in her pocket, her fingers trembling. "Now, after what just happened with Taylor, I think I really may be in danger."

"Maybe you should call the police."

"And tell them what?"

"Why you think someone wanted to harm you."

"They'll ask what proof I have, and there

isn't any. If they ask if I suspect someone, I'd have to tell them I don't know. They'll go away thinking I'm some kind of nutcase."

Maxwell didn't answer for a moment. Finally he said, "Have you told me everything about what's behind this? I get the feeling you haven't."

Emily whipped the rubber band from her curls, heedless of the sharp pricks when stray hairs snagged and were pulled. She blindly shoved the rubber band back at Maxwell, ducking her head to allow the curtain of hair to fall between them.

Hugging her seclusion around her like a comforting blanket, she answered, "I've told you enough. That's all I can say for now."

"All you are able to say, or all you want to say? There's a difference."

As Emily hesitated, Maxwell climbed awkwardly to his feet and stretched a hand toward her. "You can trust me, Emily," he said.

Emily grasped his hand and stood. Maxwell's hand was warm and firm, and for a moment his touch gave her a burst of the courage she needed. But once on her feet she quickly pulled her hand away. She couldn't trust Maxwell. She couldn't trust anyone. Not when she couldn't even trust her own childhood memories, which had been deeply buried, hiding the truth.

CHAPTER 14

I nod intelligently as our various staff members discuss study helps for our students. I even make my own contributions. I could have done that in my sleep, but I'm shaken to the core. Since the — the incident — I haven't been able to properly focus on anything else.

I hadn't meant to kill Amelia Foxworth. I was angry and frightened, and I reacted without thinking. Amelia had found out. She told me she'd publicize the résumé I had — shall we say — embellished. She was going to destroy the exemplary reputation I was building for myself and ruin my career.

I suppose subconsciously I realized that I had no choice but to stop her. It was quick. Immediate. I had not planned it. Her death was not premeditated. Desperate, frightened by Amelia's threat, I simply acted. Pushed her. Watched her fall over the railing along the marble stairs to crack her head open on the tile by the pool.

Emily saw her fall. Out of shock she's repressed her childhood memories, but someday they'll be bound to return. I can't take the chance.

When I discovered the little girl's presence, I tried to stop her, to call her back. What I would have done, if she had obeyed me, I sincerely do not know. During the months I unsuccessfully tried to discover her identity and find her, I acted blindly. I made no real plans.

This time the situation was entirely different. I did make plans — at least of a sort. I intended to seclude myself near the small dock. If Emily Wood arrived while I was there I would consider it an omen and know I must act.

So I did.

How could I know it would not be Emily who came, but another student who resembled Emily? Also, how would it have been possible to anticipate that someone else would arrive soon behind her? Just like the first time, I was so fearful, I was afraid my heart would stop beating. It was amazing that I escaped without being discovered.

It was also fortunate that the girl I had struck with a rock did not die.

But Emily Wood must die. She is a real threat to my future career and well-being. I am forced to take some type of action against her. Something that will not incriminate me.

What will it be?

CHAPTER 15

Emily slipped into a seat in the back row of the meeting hall, Maxwell beside her. Dr. Anderson, standing at a podium at the front of the room, was talking about taking responsibility. The last thing in the world Emily wanted to hear about was taking responsibility, so she scrunched down and ducked her head, letting her hair fall. There was so much to think about, to wonder about. *What if someone . . .* , she thought, but could go no further.

She suddenly realized that chairs were being scraped across the floor and people around her were rising.

"Emily Wood," a girl said, and stretched to reach Emily, handing her a folded sheet of paper.

Wordlessly, Emily took the paper, staring after the girl, who had disappeared back into the crowd.

"Aren't you going to read it?" Maxwell asked, curiosity tingeing his words.

Emily slowly opened the sheet and scanned it. "It's a note from Dr. Isaacson," she said. "He wants me to meet him in his office after this session is over."

"It's over now."

Emily gulped down the lump that rose in her throat as she pictured Dr. Isaacson's office, in which hung the portrait of Dr. Amelia Foxworth.

Maxwell stood and grasped Emily's hand, pulling her to her feet. Then he turned her hand palm up and stared at it. "Your hand's all sticky and sweaty," he said. "What's the matter?"

"I — uh — don't want to talk to Dr. Isaacson," Emily answered. She couldn't give Maxwell the real reason.

"Why not? It's not like going to the principal for something you've done wrong. This whole camp thing is supposed to be about self-esteem, so he's not going to make you feel bad about yourself. He's probably holding individual meetings with each of the people here."

Maxwell let go of Emily's hand and wiped his own hands on his jeans. "Talk about whatever he wants to talk about. Just don't shake hands with him," he added.

Emily couldn't tell Maxwell about her dread of seeing that portrait again and of trying to explain her reaction to Dr. Isaacson. Instead she said, "He may want to talk about why I fainted."

"You fainted?"

"In his office."

Maxwell groaned. "One more thing I didn't know about. Tell me. Why did you faint in his office?"

Emily looked away. "Mrs. Jimenez said it was because I was hungry. I was in her clinic. That's why I didn't come in to dinner."

Maxwell's gaze was so intense that Emily couldn't keep from meeting it. "Why do I get the idea that there's even more to that story than you've told me?" he asked.

Emily put a hand on his arm. "Don't ask me now, Maxwell. Please. I can't talk about it."

Maxwell nodded, suddenly solemn. "Okay." He glanced around the nearly empty room. "If it will make you feel better, I'll walk to his office with you."

"Thanks," Emily said. She tried to convince herself that she had nothing to be afraid of. She had her excuse. Mrs. Jimenez had given it to her.

"I was hungry," she told Dr. Isaacson a few minutes later as she perched stiffly on the edge of the loveseat in his office. As soon as he had indicated where they would talk, she had chosen the spot, making sure that the portrait was behind her. Although it was creepy to have Dr. Foxworth's portrait looking down at her, at least Emily wouldn't have to see it.

"We try to provide more than sufficient food for our students," Dr. Isaacson said. "Had you skipped lunch and breakfast?"

"No," Emily admitted.

He leaned back in his chair and smiled. Emily knew he was trying to put her at ease by making her think this was nothing more than a friendly chat. But a friendly chat wasn't possible. He was the famous psychologist-director of the Foxworth-Isaacson Educational Center, and Emily was . . . was a witness to Dr. Foxworth's death. She shivered.

"Is the air-conditioning set too low?" he asked. "I can easily adjust it for your comfort."

"No, sir. I'm fine," Emily said.

"You're fully recovered from your fainting spell?"

"It wasn't exactly a spell. I was just hungry," Emily repeated. "Mrs. Jimenez said so."

"So she reported," he said. Then abruptly, catching Emily off guard, he added, "I was informed at our staff meeting that you exhibited an interest in Dr. Amelia Foxworth."

Emily swallowed hard. It was suddenly difficult to breathe. "I just asked who she was. I saw her picture. She looked familiar." *I've said too much,* she thought. Ducking her head, she let her hair fall forward.

"Then I assume you had met Dr. Foxworth?"

"No," Emily said.

"Your parents had not brought you to the center?"

"No," Emily quickly repeated, thankful that she could answer truthfully.

His voice was low. "You said her portrait looked familiar, yet you have no early memories of Dr. Foxworth?"

Emily couldn't answer. She attempted to shrug, but it ended in another shiver.

"That thermostat definitely needs adjusting," Dr. Isaacson said. Emily heard him get to his feet and peeked out from under her hair to watch him do something with the thermostat, then return to his chair.

Squeezing her hands together tightly, Emily asked, "Why are you asking me about Dr. Foxworth?"

Dr. Isaacson's eyes widened in surprise.

"I was trying to put you at ease through friendly conversation before I got to the point of your visit." He paused before he continued. "We try to help our students reach their individual potential, so we stress individuality. In your case we hope to help you see that there is no need for you to feel you must match the individual talents of your older sisters. You can learn to discover your own talents and expand your own horizons."

He seemed to be waiting for a response, so Emily nodded, although she wondered why so many teachers, and now Dr. Isaacson, had come to the conclusion that she felt she had to match what Angela and Monica had done. She loved her sisters. She was proud of them. But she didn't want to be like them. She couldn't be. The idea of being noticed, of being on a stage — the center of attention — that was what she hated and avoided.

Dr. Isaacson said, "Taylor Farris apparently had her hair bleached and curled to match your hairstyle. Was there a reason for this?"

"No!" Emily raised her head defensively, trying to sit taller, and brushed her hair back from her face.

"Had you planned this project together?"

"No, sir," Emily answered. "She surprised me."

"Did she tell you why she made an attempt to look like you?"

"She liked my hair."

He frowned a little, as if the answer didn't satisfy him, so Emily tried to think of an answer that would. "Taylor told me she likes the way my hair falls around my face."

"And you can hide behind it."

"Yes. Oh. I mean . . ." Emily stopped. She felt herself blushing.

"You're aware that you use your hair like a shield against the world?"

"Yes, sir."

Dr. Isaacson smiled. "Good," he said. "Being aware of your reason for doing something you wish to change is the first step toward making that change. You're a bright girl, Emily, and while you're here at Camp Excel we'll help you discover abilities and talents you didn't realize you had."

He paused, but when she didn't answer, he asked, "Where do you think you can excel, Emily?"

Startled, Emily blurted out, "Why do I have to excel? Why can't I just be me?"

"You have a good mind. You have potential and the ability to excel, once you believe in yourself and find the direction you need to take. Will you let us help you?"

"Yes," Emily said. She had no choice but to give him the answer he obviously wanted.

"Do come to any of the staff if you have a problem or a question, and you'll have our undivided attention. Many of our teachers, such as Dr. Hampton and Dr. Anderson, were with our educational center when it opened and helped develop our unique and highly successful approach to learning."

"Thank you," Emily said, recognizing that the discussion was over.

"And please remember to eat properly," he said. "We want you to feel well. No more fainting spells."

He stood, smiling, and Emily obediently got to her feet.

She left his office quickly, feeling eyes staring at her back. Were they Dr. Isaacson's eyes or the glazed eyes in Dr. Amelia Foxworth's portrait? Why had Dr. Isaacson questioned her about remembering Dr. Foxworth? What did he and the rest of his staff, who obviously shared everything they heard and saw, know?

This is too much for me to handle by myself, Emily thought. *I need help.*

Maxwell, Haley, and Taylor were waiting for Emily in the lobby. Taylor's newly blond hair had been cropped short, a thick gauze pad taped to the back of her head.

Taylor struck a model's pose and said, "Ta-da! No concussion, no problems, and not much hair left. How do you like the new me?"

Stricken with guilt, Emily said, "Oh, Taylor!"

"It's not so bad," Taylor said, "although it's going to take forever for my hair to grow, especially where they shaved it in the back. Why'd I have to be so clumsy?"

Emily felt a tear roll down her cheek, and she angrily brushed it away. "Taylor, what happened to you was not your fault," she said. "It was my fault."

"I didn't tell her what you told me," Maxwell said to Emily.

"Tell me what?" Taylor asked.

Haley's eyes widened, and she asked, "Tell her what? What in the world are we talking about?"

"About what really happened to Taylor," Emily said.

Still shaken by her conversation with Dr. Isaacson, Emily jumped as a hand was placed on her shoulder and a voice spoke close to her ear. "Is everyone all right?"

Emily pulled away, gasping.

Dr. Lydia Hampton stepped back, saying,

"Oh, dear. I'm sorry. I didn't mean to startle you, Emily."

"I'm okay," Emily managed to say. She wondered if Dr. Hampton had overheard their conversation and would ask about it. Nervously, knowing her voice was too high-pitched, Emily began to babble. "We were talking about Taylor's new look. Short hair. You know. Curly around her face. Except in back, which isn't really around her face. I mean . . ."

Dr. Hampton put an arm around Emily's shoulders, as if to steady her, and said to Taylor, "I'm so sorry about what happened to you today. Thank goodness Maxwell was on hand to pull you from the water."

"Yeah. He saved my life, like in the movies or on TV," Taylor said happily. "He's my hero."

Maxwell tugged his cap farther down over his eyebrows and ears. "I just happened to be at the right place at the right time," he said.

"You were very brave and did exactly the right thing," Dr. Hampton told him. She bent her head to look down at Emily. "How about you, Emily? Are you feeling better now?"

Realizing that she was beginning to sound like a recording, Emily repeated, "I was just hungry."

"So Mrs. Jimenez said." There was a pause; then Dr. Hampton asked, "How did you like Dr. Isaacson's beautiful office? The decorator had scarcely finished by the time Camp Excel was ready to open."

Nodding agreement, Emily said, "It *is* beautiful. Especially the tapestry and the flowers."

"I personally like the cozy seating arrangement at the other end of the room," Dr. Hampton said. She smiled as she added, "I'm not too fond of those large formal portraits hanging there, however. Too imposing. It might have been nice to have still-life paintings. Flowers and fruits. What do you think?"

Emily's face grew hot. Embarrassed, she just shrugged and said, "Whatever."

Dr. Hampton turned to the others. "The portraits are of the founders of the educational center, Dr. Isaacson and his partner, Dr. Amelia Foxworth. I wish you could have met Dr. Foxworth," she said, and Emily felt Dr. Hampton's fingers tighten on her shoulder. "She was a wonderful educator who would have had a great deal to offer if she had lived."

"What happened to her?" Taylor asked.

"Dr. Foxworth died in a tragic fall," Dr. Hampton said.

"Like I almost did," Taylor said.

"Yes, I suppose there were certain similarities." She patted Emily's shoulder and looked at each in turn. "Please be careful while you're here at camp. It's very important that our — that Dr. Isaacson's theories about achievement in education be made public so that the work done by him — and the staff, of course — will get the recognition it deserves. A serious accident that would detract from the success of Camp Excel would be deeply regretted."

Emily realized that she wasn't the only one who didn't know how to answer. Silently, they watched Dr. Hampton leave, and Emily wondered if Dr. Hampton had been truly concerned for their welfare, or if they had just been given a warning. Why had she spoken about Dr. Foxworth and her portrait?

Haley leaned close. "I found a wonderful purification rite," she said. "Let's go back to the room. There is no time like the present."

"Now?" Emily asked.

"Now," Haley said.

"What's a purification rite?" Taylor asked.

"A ceremony. A charm. A way to protect Emily from evil," Haley answered.

"How about me?" Taylor asked. "I'm the

one who got my head bashed open."

"I suppose we can include you, too," Haley said. "I got the ritual from a *curandero*'s Web site, and it didn't say anything about being for just one person."

"I want to be there, too," Maxwell said.

"Yes," Emily said. "You can come with us. But before we get into whatever it is Haley wants us to do, there is something I have to tell you."

"What?" Taylor asked.

"Not here," Emily said. Although she looked from side to side and saw that no one else was nearby, she lowered her voice. "In our room."

A few minutes later, after Maxwell and Taylor had been given the chairs and Emily and Haley had perched on the bed, Emily said, "I have never told anyone, even my parents, that I have no memories at all of the year I was eight years old."

"Weird," Haley said.

"But now memories have been coming back to me. Bad memories. Horrible memories." She told them about the nightmares and about Dr. Amelia Foxworth's death and remembering the voices before her fall.

"What were the voices saying?" Taylor asked.

"I couldn't make out the words. Maybe I wasn't trying to. But I knew they were arguing. Then I saw her fall. And then there was a flash of light. For a few minutes I couldn't see."

"What do you mean, a flash of light?" Maxwell asked. "Like lightning?"

"No. It wasn't raining. There was no thunder. It was just a bright flash, right in my face." Emily shuddered and clapped her hands over her eyes. "I think Dr. Foxworth was pushed, and someone here is afraid that I'm going to tell what I know."

Haley gasped. "Are you saying she was murdered?"

"I think so." Emily told them about the voice calling to her, " 'Don't leave! Come back here!' " To her amazement the rest became clear. "And it warned, 'I'll find you! I'll find you!' " she said.

"Could you recognize the voice?" Maxwell asked.

"No," Emily said. "It was low, like a stage whisper. I'm sure whoever it was didn't want anyone else to hear."

"Was it a man's voice? Or a woman's?"

"I have no idea."

"This happened at the educational center?"

"I'm not positive, but I'm pretty sure it did." Emily slowly shook her head as she looked at Taylor. "I think you were hit on the head and pushed into the water. I think because from the back you looked like me, whoever did it thought they were getting rid of me."

Wide-eyed, Taylor reached up and touched the gauze pad at the back of her head. "Who did it?" she asked.

Emily groaned and said, "I don't know."

"Maybe we should call the police," Taylor said.

Emily sighed and said, "Maxwell thought we should, too, but I'll tell you what I told him. We have no proof of anything that happened and no suspects. The police won't pay attention to us. We have only questions without answers."

"I have a question," Maxwell said. "If you were only eight years old when you saw Dr. Foxworth fall, then you were too young to have gone to the center by yourself. How did you get there?"

"My mother said she had taken me with her when she went to visit a friend. The friend's daughter was just a year or two older than I was. I must have gone to the center with her."

"I think you should find out if that's what happened," Maxwell said. "Not knowing how and why you were there is like trying to put a puzzle together when some of the pieces are missing."

"I haven't seen the girl since then."

"Do you remember her name?"

"Yes," she said. "My mother talked about her friend, Patty Foswick, and her daughter Jamie."

"Do you know the Foswicks' address or phone number?" Maxwell asked.

"I suppose I could call my mother and ask her," Emily said. "But I'd be afraid someone in the office would hear me make the call, and pretty soon the whole staff would know about it. They tell each other everything."

Haley threw herself on her stomach, reached down to the floor near the foot of the bed, and rummaged through her handbag until she found what she was looking for. Sitting up, she handed Emily her cell phone. "My mother made me bring this," she said. "I'm supposed to call her every day."

"Do you?" Taylor asked.

"Don't bug me," Haley said. "We're here to talk about Emily, not me."

Emily checked her watch, relieved to see that it wasn't too late to call. Her parents would be about to turn on the ten o'clock news. She dialed, and before the third ring her mother answered.

"Hi, Mom," Emily said.

"Darling!" Mrs. Wood answered. "How are you? We've missed you." Then her voice deepened. "Emily, love," she said, "you aren't calling to ask to come home, are you, because you know that your father and I —"

I can tell Mom all about the nightmares and what happened to Taylor and everything I suspect, Emily thought. *My mother wouldn't let anything terrible happen to me.* "Oh, Mom," she began, but she stopped abruptly, realizing that her mother would tell her father, and they'd call the school to find out what was going on, and everyone on the staff would know that Emily was about to blow the whistle.

If the murderer of Dr. Foxworth was determined to keep Emily from talking, her time on earth would be numbered in minutes. There was no way she could involve her parents.

"Mom," Emily said, "I only called to ask if you still have a phone number for your friend in Dallas, Patty Foswick."

"Yes, I do," Mrs. Wood told her. "But tell me why in the world you want her phone number."

"I don't want her number exactly," Emily

said. "I want her daughter Jamie's." She fumbled for the right way to explain. "There's somebody here who hasn't seen her for years and wants to talk to her."

"Oh, that's sweet," Mrs. Wood said. "Hang on one minute and I'll get it for you."

Emily jumped off the bed, leaned across Taylor, and reached into her desk for a pencil and paper. When her mother returned with the phone number she was ready and wrote it down.

"Tell me everything you've been doing, sweetheart," Mrs. Wood said.

Emily said, "Mom, that would take forever, and it's late. I've got to go. Okay?"

"Well . . . okay," her mother said. "We miss you, Emily. We love you."

"I love you, too," Emily said. She could feel tears burning behind her eyes, and she took a deep breath, willing them away. If she'd only been allowed to spend the summer at home . . . if she hadn't been forced to come to camp . . . if she lived through this summer . . .

"Bye, Mom," Emily said firmly, and pressed the End button on the phone.

She held out the phone to Haley, but Haley shook her head. "Call your friend," she said. "You need to find out as much as you can as soon as you can."

Emily dialed the number her mother had given her.

A young voice answered, and Emily asked, "Is this Jamie?"

"Yes, it is," Jamie said. "Is this Megan? You sound different."

"My name isn't Megan," Emily answered. "I'm Emily Wood, and about eight years ago my mother and I came to spend a weekend with you and your mother. You probably don't remember me."

"Emily Wood?" The voice was questioning.

"The reason I'm calling is because I think you took me to the Foxworth-Isaacson Educational Center. I mean, I can remember climbing through some vines up to where I could see a swimming pool and —"

A burst of laughter cut Emily short. "Now I remember you. Snakes. You were scared to death that snakes and bugs would be in the underbrush."

"Where was this underbrush?"

"On the hill behind the center."

"Can you tell me more about it?"

Jamie chuckled again, then said, "I suppose I wasn't very nice to you. It was too much fun scaring you about snakes and giant tree roaches, then daring you to climb up to the top."

"Climb up what?"

"There were lots of trees on the slope, with honeysuckle vines growing wild through the branches, and in one place it made kind of a tunnel that some of the neighbor kids and I discovered. One at a time we'd climb up through the tunnel until we got to the top, and if we were real quiet and no one spotted us peeking out from under the leaves, we could spy on the people at the center who were swimming in the pool or sunbathing."

"There was a tall marble staircase next to the pool area," Emily said.

"Hey, that's right. You've got a good memory. Sorry about all I said to you then about bugs and snakes."

"It's okay. Just help me remember. What happened when I came down from the tunnel?"

There was silence for a moment; then Jamie said, "I thought you'd brag about making it all the way to the top, but you didn't say a word. You were kind of white and shaky. And then I said, 'Don't move. There's a giant tree roach on your shoulder.' Only there really wasn't. I just wanted to see you jump."

"Did I?"

"Yes, but that wasn't all you did. You

screamed. Then you ran toward our house, screaming all the way and yelling something about the cockroach, I guess — that it was going to find you. Your mom got you calmed down, and I confessed to scaring you about the make-believe roach, and my mom made me apologize."

"Did I say anything about where I'd been or what I was doing . . . or what I'd seen?"

"Not a word. You didn't rat on me, if that's what you're asking." Again Jamie laughed. "Is that why you called me after all these years? Do you want another apology?"

"No," Emily said. "I was just talking with friends about not remembering things, and I thought you could fill in some of the blanks."

"Did I?"

"Yes, you did. Thanks." Then Emily asked, "Did you go back to spy again?"

"Funny you should ask that. No, we didn't. We couldn't. Maybe *you* owe *us* an apology. The people at the center must have seen or heard you. Someone put boards across that area and ended our spying."

"I'm sorry," Emily said.

"Hey, just kidding."

"Well, thanks, Jamie," Emily said again. "Bye."

As she handed the phone back to Haley,

Emily repeated to the others everything Jamie had said.

"That means you never told anyone what you had seen," Maxwell said. "But someone there saw you — even called after you to come back and warned they'd find you."

"And they did." Taylor looked solemnly at Emily.

"It might help if we knew which members of the staff here at camp were working at the center in Dallas eight years ago," Maxwell said.

"We know who some of them were," Emily said.

"That's not enough. We have to know every name," Maxwell said.

"Can't you just ask them?" Taylor suggested.

"No," Maxwell said. "We can't say anything about this to anyone."

"Then how do we find out?" Taylor asked.

"I think we'll have to find a way to ask that won't seem suspicious," Emily answered. "We can't just come right out and say, 'Where were you eight years ago?' "

"The staff tell each other everything about us," Maxwell reminded her.

"We can each try to think of an idea," Emily said. She turned to Maxwell. "You're a writer. What would a writer do to get information?"

Maxwell tugged his cap downward with both hands as he said, "I'm not just a writer, I'm a *playwright*. I don't interview people, and I don't write biographies."

"Okay, okay," Emily said. "But try to think about what we *can* do to get the information. Everybody think of something."

Haley slid off the bed and stood. "All right. We'll all try to come up with something by tomorrow morning," she said. "Now that we've got that taken care of, we'd better face facts."

Slowly, she looked at each in turn. "This is the desperate moment Loki has been warning us about. It should be clear to everyone that Em needs protection from evil. It's time to hold our purification rite."

CHAPTER 16

I have decided upon the place where it will happen.

I know the time and date.

All I need now is to work out the details. That shouldn't be difficult.

CHAPTER 17

Haley closed the blinds, making sure they were snug and no one could see inside. Then she arranged a semicircle by placing one of the desk chairs between the two beds. Maxwell was given the chair, while Emily and Taylor sat opposite each other on the edges of the twin beds.

"We need an altar table," Haley said. She glanced around the room for what she might find, gathered up a few books, and placed them in a stack on one of her suitcases. On top of the stack she centered a fat, stubby, yellowish candle that looked to Emily like nothing more than a glob of lard. Holding a book of matches in one hand and a small paper packet in the other, she stood facing Maxwell, completing the circle.

"Give me your vial of potion," she told Emily, who reached into her pocket, pulled it out, and handed it to Haley.

"What's that stuff? It looks like ink," Taylor said.

"It's a special potion to protect Emily," Haley answered. "She has to keep it on her person at all times — except now, during this purification rite," she quickly added.

"Who said so?"

"A *curandero*."

"What's a —"

"A healer who can foresee the future," Haley impatiently answered. "No more questions. Pay attention."

She closed her eyes, paused as if making sure the others would be silent, and intoned in a low voice, "The circle is a symbol of protection from harm. Our circle must not be broken."

"Where'd you get that awful-looking candle?" Taylor whispered. "It looks like it's going to smell terrible."

Haley glared at Taylor. "I bought it from the *curandero* in Lampley when Emily and I were there. He blessed it himself. It has magical powers. And that's all I'm going to say before we get back to the rite. From now on, don't interrupt."

"Sorry," Taylor mumbled.

"I said, don't interrupt!"

Taylor opened her mouth as if she was going to answer, then seemed to think better of it and closed her lips together tightly.

If Haley had tried this ceremony yesterday, Emily thought, she would have left the room in a hurry, wanting no part of any of Haley's dramatics. But tonight, still frightened by the memories that had poured back into her mind, knowing that her nightmares had not been make-believe, Emily huddled with the others, glad they were nearby. After all that had happened, she was terrified of being alone.

Haley began to chant in a singsong voice. The words were in Spanish, and Emily had studied French in school, not Spanish, but a few of the words were familiar: *cuidado, peligro, muerte* . . . caution, danger, death. Emily shivered, and Haley nodded at her approvingly.

"You're feeling the power. It's starting to work," Haley whispered. She opened the packet, sprinkling a small amount of granules around the top of the candle. Then she struck a match and lit the candle.

As she turned out the light in the room, the incense granules caught, sending up both a swirl of smoke and an overpowering fragrance as sticky sweet as marshmallows.

Emily began to cough, and Maxwell rubbed his eyes, trying to shift his chair back, away from the smoke.

"Don't move! Don't you dare break the

circle!" Haley ordered.

Maxwell froze.

Haley carefully opened Emily's vial of potion and tipped a drop onto her right thumb. She pressed her thumb against Emily's forehead. As she repeated this performance with Maxwell and Taylor, Emily could see the dark smudge Haley's potion-wet thumb had left on the others and knew she'd have a similar blob on her own face.

The damp spot on her forehead felt like a crystal of ice burning into her skin. She wanted to rub it away but didn't dare.

She saw Taylor wince and Maxwell begin to reach up to rub away the stain, then apparently change his mind, so Emily realized she wasn't the only one who felt the strange burning sensation. What had the *curandero* mixed with the liquid? Hot peppers? Nettles?

Emily stared at the vial in disgust. There was no telling what the *curandero* had used to make this black, evil-looking stuff, which he could bottle and sell as some kind of magic to superstitious, unsuspecting customers like Haley . . . and her.

Haley corked the vial, reached over, and tucked it back into Emily's pocket. In spite of her misgivings, Emily didn't protest. She surprised herself by feeling strangely comforted that the vial had been returned.

Haley enfolded her thumb in her other hand and rubbed it, as if the stinging potion was bothering her, too. Then she pulled a small, creased sheet of paper from her shirt pocket, opened it, and began to read from it, holding it close to the candlelight. " 'May only that which is good and pure dwell within our bodies, so that which is good and pure in the world around us shall protect us from evil. May our healing goodness protect us from the arrows of destruction that fly against us. May our enemies be defeated and our victories be proclaimed. May the healing potion with which we have been anointed burn away all desires for wrong-doing within us, leaving only truth and beauty in their place. May we all —' "

With a sudden sputter, the candle flickered and went out, leaving the room in darkness.

While Haley fumbled for the light switch, Taylor called, "Hey, who did that?"

"None of us," Maxwell answered.

Emily squinted in the sudden bright overhead light. A thin spiral of dark smoke rose from the hollow in the candle in which a few threads of the wick lay. "No one touched the candle," she said. "I was watching it when it went out."

Haley flopped onto the floor in front of them and clapped her hands to her cheeks. Her face was pale, and her eyes showed her fear. "The candle wasn't supposed to do that," she said. "It was an omen. A bad omen."

Taylor reached over to pat her shoulder. "It was a nice ceremony, though, what there was of it," she said.

"We hadn't finished it," Haley complained. "We were just coming to the part where we banish all evil spirits."

"Can't we light the candle again and keep going?" Taylor asked.

Maxwell picked up the candle and poked his finger into the melted wax. "No," he said. "There's no more wick."

"Bummer," Taylor said.

"It wasn't supposed to be like that," Haley said. "The rite was supposed to protect Emily."

"And now it won't?"

"I don't know."

I don't believe in all this anyhow, Emily reminded herself. There was really no reason for her to feel upset, for her heart to beat a little faster, and for her hands to sweat. She wiped her hands down the sides of her shorts. "I suppose it will have to be up to us," she said.

Haley looked up at her. "Well, yes. You have your potion to protect you, and —"

"I mean we'll have to rely on ourselves and what we can find out and not depend on ceremonies and potions." Emily knew that the smile she gave Taylor was a little shaky, but at least her voice was firm. "If I'm not alone, if I'm always with someone . . ." She took a deep breath and went on. "Taylor, Haley . . . could one of you hang out with me, like when I go to class or meals?"

They both hurried to agree, and Maxwell chimed in. "One of us will be with you at all times," he said. "At least until we figure out what is going on and have enough information to inform the police."

"Should we tell Dr. Isaacson everything I told you?" Emily asked. "I mean, he's in charge. He should know what we think is taking place. Maybe he could even help us."

"Unless he's the one who's threatening you," Maxwell said.

Emily remembered Dr. Isaacson's searching questions about if and how she had known Dr. Foxworth. "Then I guess we'll keep everything to ourselves for a while," she said.

Maxwell peered out from under his cap. "Will you be okay until morning?"

"Of course she will. I'll be with her," Haley said.

A sharp rap on the door made Emily jump. Taylor let out a shriek.

Haley inched the door open, then widened it as she saw Tammy Johnson, another camper, standing there. "Oh, it's you," she said, relief in her voice.

"You promised you'd meet me in the lobby and go over my essay with me," Tammy said.

"Oh," Haley said. "I forgot."

"Well, could you come now?"

Emily couldn't help seeing the worried expression on Tammy's face. "Go ahead," she told Haley.

Haley glanced at Taylor and Maxwell. "You're sure?"

"I'm sure," Emily said.

Tammy pointed at Maxwell. "How come he's in your room? There's a rule. Guys aren't supposed to be in the girls' rooms."

"He's just leaving," Emily said.

As Haley slipped out of the room, shutting the door behind her, Maxwell said, "Maybe I should stay."

"No. Tammy was right. You shouldn't break the rules. We don't want you to get into trouble," Emily said.

"I'm not worried about getting into

trouble. I may have mentioned that a play-wright grows and learns his craft through life's varied experiences."

"Good night, Maxwell," Emily said firmly.

She watched Maxwell leave, then summoned all her courage and said to Taylor, "You don't have to stay just because Haley took off."

"It's okay," Taylor said. "I'll get my notebook and be right back. I want to work on my English assignment." As she stepped into the hall, she said, "I'll be back in two minutes." She quietly shut the door.

Emily opened her notebook and found a pencil that didn't need sharpening. Next she returned the two chairs to their places by the desks. She wondered where Taylor had gone. She'd said she would be right back.

Pulling one of the chairs out, Emily sat on it, but her back was to the door, and it made her feel creepy, so she moved to sit on the edge of the bed again. *I'm hiding,* she thought. *Ever since Dr. Foxworth's murder, I've been hiding.* The realization didn't surprise her. She guessed that she must always have known that her refusal to become the center of attention was not because she felt she couldn't compete with her older sisters' achievements. That was a separate problem with which she'd have to deal. But the hiding, even behind her mass of curly hair, was because she had been terribly afraid that whoever had threatened her really would find her.

For a moment she thought she heard footsteps in the hall . . . someone breathing . . . listening . . . the doorknob turning. What was keeping Taylor?

When at last a soft knock came, Emily stiffened. "Come on in," she tried to call to Taylor, but her voice came out in a rough croak, and she had to start over.

The door opened, but the person standing there wasn't Taylor. It was Mrs. Comstock.

"Emily, I hope you don't mind a quick visit," Mrs. Comstock said. "I noticed your roommate in the dorm lobby studying with Tammy Johnson. I knew you'd be alone for a little while and we could talk. May I come in?"

"Um — sure," Emily said. She stood, tense, scared, and ready to run as Mrs. Comstock stepped into the room and shut the door, leaning against it.

Run? There was no way she could escape. Mrs. Comstock was blocking the only exit.

Emily could hear her heart beating in her

ears, and she felt her palms grow sticky with sweat. Probably no one had seen Mrs. Comstock enter the room, and she'd be sure that no one would see her leave. If something happened to Emily, there would be no witnesses. "What do you want to talk about?" Emily managed to ask.

"First of all, I want to make sure that you're feeling well." Mrs. Comstock took a step closer to Emily. "No more dizziness? No more feeling faint?"

Emily shook her head and repeated her excuse. "Mrs. Jimenez said I was just hungry."

Mrs. Comstock smiled. "Hungry . . . or stressed? I'm more inclined to think it was the latter."

Emily took a step back. "What do you mean?"

"You're in an unfamiliar place, away from the protection of your family."

Protection? Emily flinched. Why had she used that word?

Mrs. Comstock had taken another step toward Emily, but she stopped and silently studied Emily's face. "If something here at Camp Excel has disturbed you, perhaps it would help if you'd confide in one of the staff," she began. "You can talk to me, Emily. I'm your friend. I want to —"

The door burst open, and Taylor flew into the room, blue-black smudges outlining her eyes. Emily gave a cry of relief at seeing her, but Mrs. Comstock stumbled back, trying to get out of the way.

"I'm sorry I took so long," Taylor said in a rush. She stopped as she saw Mrs. Comstock and looked at her inquisitively.

"Hello, Taylor," Mrs. Comstock said.

"Hi," Taylor said. "I didn't know you were here. I thought the teachers —"

"Slept in their classrooms?" Mrs. Comstock finished the sentence and laughed.

Taylor looked indignant. "That's not what I was going to say," she answered.

Mrs. Comstock stepped around her to reach the door, then paused and looked at Emily. "Tomorrow afternoon is our field trip to the Longhorn Cavern," she said. "I want to make certain you feel well enough to take the walk through the cave. It takes at least an hour and a half."

"I feel fine. I can do it," Emily told her.

Mrs. Comstock smiled. "Good," she said. "The cavern is fascinating. I'd hate to have you miss it."

The moment she left, Taylor slammed her notebook onto Haley's desk and said, "I wasn't going to say that teachers sleep in their classrooms. Does she think I'm in first grade?"

Emily didn't have a chance to answer before Taylor went on. "And I hate her dumb idea about making us go down into a big hole in the ground. What was she doing prowling around the dorm anyhow? The teachers were all supposed to be at something called an 'end-of-day wrap-up.' I saw the note on the bulletin board over in the main building."

Calming down, she picked up her notebook and asked, "By the way, have you got an extra pencil? I got to talking to my roommate and forgot to bring mine."

"You didn't tell her about . . . you know . . . about what we were talking about, did you?"

"Of course not," Taylor said. "We were talking about makeup. She bought some new eyeliner that's really cool."

"You're wearing it."

Taylor giggled. "Sure. I had to see what it would look like on me." She went on describing her roommate's makeup purchase, but Emily tuned her out. She suspected that Mrs. Comstock had come to the room because she knew Emily would be alone. Had she really been worried that Emily wouldn't feel well enough to hike an hour and a half through the cavern? Or did she have another purpose?

I'm scared, Emily admitted to herself. *I don't know what's going to happen next, and I'm really scared.*

CHAPTER 18

My plans for Emily's termination are easily falling into place, and I will have a perfect alibi.

Her death will be a sad note but will in no way intrude upon the success of Camp Excel, and the recognition of the work that will enhance my career.

So sorry, Emily, but I have no other choice.

CHAPTER 19

At some moment during the very early morning hours, a lone mockingbird trilled exuberantly to a still-dark sky, waking Emily. An idea unfolded in her mind, and she sighed with relief. Before she slipped back into sleep, she knew what she must do.

She kept her plan to herself until Haley had finished her meditation, drawn her rune, and happily proclaimed, "V — Vara. Ahhh! I drew the rune of love."

"You're going to fall in love?" Emily asked. "With someone here at camp?"

Haley rolled her eyes. "Not so you'd notice," she said. "Besides, if you draw the Vara symbol it doesn't mean you'll fall in love. Vara was a goddess who escorted the souls of the ancient Norse warriors to Valhalla. That was Viking heaven. Drawing her rune just means that happiness will be found."

"Happiness would be nice," Emily said.

Haley held out the box of stones. "Don't

175

you want to draw a rune? It might make you feel better."

"No, thanks. I feel fine," Emily told Haley.

"But chances are you'll get a *good* forecast this time, and we can all stop worrying about you."

"Just like that?"

"Well, why not? The runes know your future for today."

"So do I. Today I'm going to start my project for English class."

Haley looked surprised. "You've got an idea already? I get my best ideas the day before they're due." She stepped into the closet to place her box of runes on the shelf.

Emily asked, "Don't you want to hear my idea?"

Haley reappeared and sat on the bed, her shoes in her hands. "Go ahead," she said.

"I'm going to put together a directory made up of interviews with the staff about their studies and careers."

"Bor-ing." Haley made a face before she bent over to tie the laces on her sneakers.

"Don't you know why?" Emily asked. "It will give me the excuse I need to find out who was working at the center eight years ago and then ask questions that might help me figure out who might have argued with

Dr. Foxworth and pushed her off the stairs and why."

Haley sat up, looking surprised. "Oh. What if they catch on to why you're asking questions? Especially the one who . . ." She stopped, unable to finish.

"I'll hope they won't."

"Doesn't that scare you?"

"Yes."

"Then why are you going to do it?"

"It's the only way I can think of to find out who also hit Taylor and who might be trying to harm me."

Haley spoke slowly. "Maybe what happened to Taylor really was only an accident."

Emily pulled the vial from the pocket of her shorts. She kept her eyes on Haley. "Then I won't need this," she said.

"Yes, you will!" Haley jumped to her feet. "Put that back in your pocket!"

"Haley, believing in this potion is only superstition," Emily said.

Haley shook her head. "You're wrong. It's no more superstition than my runes are."

Emily didn't want to argue. Without another word she slipped the vial back into her pocket.

Haley, satisfied that she had convinced Emily, flipped back her hair and said,

"Ready for breakfast?"

"Ready," Emily said. She followed Haley to the door. "Want to help me interview the staff?"

"Me?" Haley looked astonished. "I don't know how to interview people. Besides, it's not *my* class project. It's *yours,* and Dr. Weil said he wants our projects to be original and individual. Come on. Let's hurry. I'm absolutely starving to death."

As soon as they had filled their trays, Emily saw Taylor wave to them from one of the tables on the opposite side of the room, so they joined her.

Emily saw no sign of Maxwell, but he appeared at her side the moment she and Taylor left for their first class, history. Emily told them about her plan to interview the staff.

"That sounds like a lot of work," Taylor said. She smiled to herself. "I'm going to write a poem."

Maxwell gave Emily a knowing look. "I think you found a good way to get the information we need," he said.

"Dr. Weil said there was no word limit," Taylor added, "but I don't think the poem should be too short. He might not like it."

"I'll start the interviews this morning," Emily said.

"Good plan," Maxwell said.

"Maybe I'll write my poem in the form of an old-fashioned sonnet," Taylor said. "That should surprise him."

"Does either of you want to help me?" Emily asked.

"Help you what?" Taylor asked.

"Interview the staff for the directory I'm going to write."

Maxwell thought a moment, then said, "No. It's too obvious. Since everyone probably knows that Dr. Weil's assignment was for individual projects, it would look strange for you to bring someone with you. The person whose identity you're trying to uncover might become suspicious."

"Why don't you just write a poem?" Taylor suggested. "It's so much easier."

Emily opened the door to Mrs. Comstock's room. "Never mind," she said, knowing she sounded braver than she felt. "I'll take care of it myself."

Maxwell smiled and said, "Just remember that we're here for you, Emily."

"You know it," Taylor added.

They chose the same seats they'd had before, in the back row. But this time Emily sat up, pushing her hair back from her face, so that she could watch Mrs. Comstock carefully. The teacher often nodded vigorously to emphasize what she was saying, her short brown hair bouncing, and she smiled often. Was the smile real? Emily wondered. Or was it put on for show? She hoped she'd find out.

"Before I give you some of the historical background of the Longhorn Cavern, I want to remind you not to be late this afternoon. Meet at the main drive at four o'clock. There will be about thirty people going from Camp Excel — this class and one other — and our vans will take us to the cavern. Be on time. We'll be the last tour group of the day to be escorted through the cave, and I don't want our guide to have to stay overtime."

"Is this supposed to be a lesson in responsibility?" Maxwell whispered to Emily.

"Does it matter?" Emily asked.

"Not to me, it doesn't. Playwrights are creative individuals, unfettered by the restraints that bind other people. Can you imagine Arthur Miller breaking his creative thought by rushing to catch a van at four o'clock?"

"Let's pay attention back there," Mrs. Comstock said.

Embarrassed, Emily had all she could do to keep from ducking behind her curtain of hair. Instead, she sat taller, ignoring

Maxwell, and tried to pay attention.

"Some of you have seen pictures on television of the caves in the mountains of Afghanistan," Mrs. Comstock explained. "The Longhorn Cavern was formed much like those caves were formed, perhaps five hundred million years ago when both areas were covered by shallow seas. That is when the limestone that makes up the caves was deposited. Then, during the mountains' upheaval, which is called the Llano uplift, about two hundred eighty million years ago, water began to pour through the cracks and faults of the limestone, creating tunnels — some of them immense."

"But we're a long way from the sea," someone broke in.

"That's right," Mrs. Comstock said. "And we're a long way from two hundred and eighty million years ago. The earth never stops growing and changing."

"Now, let's talk about some of the people from our own era who made use of this cavern, such as the Comanche Indians. They were able to penetrate the main room of the cavern, which later was named the Council Room, and found layers of chert rock, or flint, with which they made arrowheads and tools."

"I don't understand," someone said.

"You said the Indians were able to penetrate the main room of the cavern. That means there were other rooms. What about them?"

"At that time most of the rooms in the cavern were filled with mud and guano," she answered.

"What's guano?"

"Dropping from the millions of Mexican free-tailed bats that once lived in the cave."

"Gross," Taylor muttered.

"Not to the Confederates who discovered the cave during the Civil War," Mrs. Comstock said. "A detachment from the Confederate army used this room to secretly manufacture gunpowder made from sulfur, charcoal, and nitrate. The nitrate came from the bat guano."

"Was this ever proved to be true?" someone asked. "Were artifacts found to support this story?"

"Yes," Mrs. Comstock answered. "In addition to information found in historical records, a number of rusted guns, bullet molds, and a bayonet were found, along with countless arrowheads. And, oh, yes, two human skeletons were found in the cave."

"Whose?"

"We don't know," she said. "There is also a legend that the notorious outlaw Sam Bass, who robbed stagecoaches and trains back in the late eighteen hundreds, hid his stolen gold in the cavern. Since no gold has ever been found, the story remains a rumor."

"Did Sam Bass bury his gold in the guano?" someone else asked, and everyone laughed.

"I doubt it," Mrs. Comstock said. "Even outlaws have sensibilities."

"None of the ones I know," Maxwell said, and the class laughed again.

Mrs. Comstock went on with her story. "In the early thirties, the state of Texas bought the cave from the gentleman on whose property the main entrance was found," she said. "The Civilian Conservation Corps sent young men to clean out the cavern. According to records kept by the organization, the boys in the CCC were paid a dollar a day and cleaned out over two and a half million cubic yards of debris."

"Yuck!" Taylor closed her eyes for a moment. "All that bat fertilizer and mud? What kind of a job was that?"

"The kind of job that kept the boys alive during the worst of the Depression years," Mrs. Comstock answered. "People were starving. They were glad of any kind of work that would provide them with food and a bed for the night." She smiled. "It wasn't all cleanup work, though. The CCC also built trails in the area, constructed the administration building and observation tower, and installed the lighting system inside the cave."

"Then could people explore all the rooms in the cave?" Maxwell asked, and Emily could see that he'd become interested in spite of himself.

"All that had been opened to the public," Mrs. Comstock answered, "and remember that the people I've told you about used the cave even before it had been thoroughly cleaned out. During Prohibition in the twenties, the owner installed a wooden dance floor in the Indian Council Room and turned it into a nightclub, or speakeasy. I understand that it became a very popular place to go to dance, eat, and drink because the cave was always cool, even in the hot summers. However, that entrance into the Indian Council Room was sealed off in the mid-thirties. The only entrance and exit to the cavern is the one near the administration building, which we'll use."

A girl in the front row raised her hand. "I've never been in a cave," she said, "but

184

I've seen lots of photographs of stalactites and stalagmites. Is that what we'll see?"

Mrs. Comstock picked up a marker and went to the board, where she drew wide swirls, circles, and S-shaped lines. "This is the type of formation you'll see in the cavern," she said. "A few stalactites and stalagmites had formed in the Indian Council Room, but during the evenings when the cave was used for dining and dancing, they were broken off by unthinking souvenir hunters. The cave's beauty is in the design of the rocks, carved by water. The cavern has a strange, surrealistic look."

Emily sat back, thinking about the cave. She had never been inside a cave, either. She supposed Mrs. Comstock was right in telling them that it was beautiful, and she had told them earlier that they'd be safe if they stayed on the paths, but there was something about being underground with only one entrance and exit that made her feel creepy. She could understand why going underground frightened Taylor.

Mrs. Comstock went on to other stories about the early settlers in the area and the exploits of Sam Bass and his gang. Emily tried to concentrate and even took notes, but she couldn't shake the uncomfortable prickle of fear that taunted her whenever she thought about descending into the cave.

When class was over, Emily hurried to stand in front of Mrs. Comstock. She held her open notebook in one arm and a pen in the other and tried to look businesslike. "Mrs. Comstock," she said in a rush, "I'm working on a project for Dr. Weil's English class. It's a directory, designed to give the kids here, and their parents, some personal information about the members of the staff at Camp Excel."

Mrs. Comstock didn't smile. She raised one eyebrow as she studied Emily. "What kind of information? How personal?"

"Oh, just normal stuff," Emily said. She poised her pen over her notebook, ready to write. "Like what's your favorite color and favorite thing to eat?"

"The color green and fried chicken," Mrs. Comstock answered.

"Great." Emily wrote so fast she was scribbling. "And where did you go to school?"

"The University of North Carolina for both my B.A. and master's."

Emily kept her gaze glued to the notebook. "Where have you taught?"

"Both public and private schools in North Carolina and then the Foxworth-Isaacson Educational Center."

"When?" The word came out so raspy Emily had to clear her throat and ask again.

"Let's see. I began teaching in 1987 and took a position at the center in 1993, when it opened."

Emily jotted down the dates, her fingers trembling. Mrs. Comstock had been at the center even longer than eight years before. She glanced up to see Mrs. Comstock looking at her quizzically. "Th-thanks," Emily stammered.

"Is that it?" Mrs. Comstock asked. "Aren't you going to ask about my hobbies or talents or clubs I belong to or anything like that?"

"Oh, yes, I am, in future interviews," Emily said. She could feel herself blushing. She should have known she wasn't asking enough questions. "Right now I have to get to English class, and I know you have another class to teach. I'll see you later. Okay?"

Mrs. Comstock smiled. "Okay. Good luck with your project."

But Emily could feel Mrs. Comstock's eyes on her back as she left the room, elbowing past the kids who were entering, and she had the weird feeling that she hadn't fooled Mrs. Comstock for a minute.

CHAPTER 20

The picture of Emily Wood has arrived. Express delivery. Alice is highly efficient.

There is no mistaking the identity of the terrified little girl in the photo. Her eyes are wide with both the horror of what she had seen and the unpleasant surprise of a camera flash right in her face. I have no doubts at all. The child is definitely Emily Wood.

I remember that the camera had been in my hands. When I heard a cry of shock and fear coming from the foliage on the hill, I scrambled down the steps toward the source. That was the first time I had noticed the tunnel-like opening in the undergrowth. And there was the child — a perfect stranger — staring at Amelia Foxworth's body. Obviously, the little girl was so horrified, she must have been unable to move. I pressed the button on the camera and took her picture. I'm glad I did. I have proof, and the proof is positive.

CHAPTER 21

Emily found Maxwell and Taylor standing in the hallway outside the classroom.

"Why'd you wait?" she asked.

"We said we'd stay with you to protect you," Taylor said.

"I'm very good at saving lives," Maxwell said. He nudged Taylor, and she giggled. "You realize, don't you, that my swift action in pulling you to safety will be a scene in one of my autobiographical plays?"

"I'll be in a play? Then I'll be famous, too!" Taylor said.

"If I remember your name," Maxwell answered. He turned to Emily. "How did your interview with Mrs. Comstock go?"

"Fine," Emily said, although she knew it hadn't. She hadn't asked enough questions or the right questions. But she thought she knew how to take care of that problem. She'd try a different approach on Dr. Weil.

A short time later, when he asked his class to volunteer to discuss their projects, Emily raised her hand. "I'm going to write a series of interviews with the staff members who were with the educational center from the time it opened," she said.

"Ah, yes. That was 1993, I do believe."

"Were you with the center then?"

"No," he said. "I had a position with the Tyler school district, with which I am still connected. I've taken this Camp Excel job for two reasons: summer employment and because I believe so wholeheartedly in Dr. Isaacson's approach to education."

Dr. Weil smiled at Emily. "Your idea has merit. I'm looking forward to reading the interviews when you've finished." He glanced around the room. "Anyone else?"

Taylor waved her hand, but so did some of the others. As they talked about what they would write, Emily sat back, relieved that her second plan had worked. She could narrow down the list of names, which would mean less interviewing and less writing. Mostly, it would mean that there would be fewer people to think about and watch out for.

Before she went to lunch she stepped into the next classroom down the hall. She didn't have Mr. Anderson for math, but he smiled at her explanation of her project. "You can write about my wife, but not me," he said, his breath reeking of stale cigarette smoke and peppermint. "Lorene was hired by Dr. Isaacson before the center opened. It's why she moved to Dallas from Indiana."

"Didn't you work there, too?"

"No. We didn't even meet until three years later. I was working with the Dallas public schools."

"But you're working at the center this summer?"

"I thought it would be a good way to spend the summer together." He chuckled. "But Lorene's been so busy setting things up and getting through the first two days that I've hardly seen her."

As Emily turned to leave his classroom, Mr. Anderson said, "Lorene's really proud of what the staff at the center have accomplished. She's sure their work will be recognized and praised by the top educators throughout the world. If you can find her, I know she'll be glad to give you more than enough information for your project."

"Thanks," Emily said. She paused as an idea popped into her mind. "Do you know which of the staff members here this summer were with the center when it opened or even a year or two after, like maybe 1995 or before?" She held her breath. Had she been too obvious?

Mr. Anderson leaned back in his chair and thought a moment. "Not many were with the center then," he said. "Let's see . . . besides Lorene, there's Gail Comstock, Dr. Lydia Hampton, Dr. Joseph Bonaduce — he teaches government and civics — and Dorothy Hill. She's chemistry and physics. I think that's it."

Emily wrote down the names, thanked him again, and left.

"I'm starving," Taylor wailed as Emily walked into the hall. "Can't we go to lunch now?"

"Go without me," Emily answered. She noticed that Taylor was alone. "Where are Haley and Maxwell?"

"Haley's eating lunch with Tammy, and Maxwell said he'd go ahead and save us seats."

"You go in and tell Maxwell that I'll be along as soon as I talk to just a few more people."

"I thought you wanted someone to stay with you," Taylor said. "I'll wait outside their rooms. I'm hungry, but I'm not *that* hungry."

Emily smiled. "Go ahead. I'll be all right. I'm tired of hiding and trying to be invisible. I've been hiding for too long," she added.

"I don't get it," Taylor said. "You're not

hiding, and you're not invisible. You're right here in the hall."

"It's a bad joke," Emily said. "Go on. Get lunch. I'll join you soon." She turned and walked down the hall, checking the names on the doors.

She reached Mrs. Hill's room just as Mrs. Hill and Dr. Bonaduce walked into the hall. Emily told them about her interview plan and asked them a few basic questions. They were polite and kind and hardly seemed like possible suspects.

But there was one more person to interview: the camp's counselor and psychiatrist, Dr. Hampton.

As Emily passed Dr. Isaacson's office, she stopped and touched the doorknob, and before she realized what had happened, the unlocked door had opened. Even though she knew she shouldn't be there, Emily stepped inside, closing the door silently behind her.

She laid her notebook on a small table near the door, then forced herself to move forward to look at Dr. Foxworth's portrait again. From a face frozen in time, glassy, vacant eyes stared back at her. A chill ran through Emily's shoulders and neck, but she found she could now face the picture without flinching. The memories this time were not from a nightmare. They were real. They were complete. Someone had argued with Dr. Foxworth. Someone had pushed her over the marble steps, and she had fallen to the tiles and died. Someone had murdered her.

Emily suddenly realized that she had walked over to Dr. Isaacson's desk, where an enlarged photograph lay in the center of some folders. Out of curiosity, Emily picked it up.

From a background of leaves and a ragged sprig of honeysuckle blossoms, Emily's own slightly younger face stared back. Her hair was a cloudy white aura framing wide, terrified eyes.

Shivering with shock and cold, Emily dropped the photo on the desktop and backed away. Now she knew that the flash of light that had blinded her had been a camera flash. The person who had killed Dr. Foxworth had heard Emily's cry of shock, had discovered her hiding place, and had taken her picture. So this was how she'd been recognized at Camp Excel.

She began to wonder why the photograph was lying on Dr. Isaacson's desk. He was the person in whom she had thought of confiding. Had he taken the photo? Was he the murderer?

Emily froze as she heard his voice in the hall. She couldn't be caught here — not with this picture in plain sight. He'd know she'd seen it.

There was a side door in the office, and she ran to it, her footsteps silent on the thick rug. As she slipped into the private bathroom, closing the door quietly behind her, she heard Dr. Isaacson enter his office, obviously upset as he talked to whoever was with him.

Inch by inch Emily quietly slid the window open. She could easily climb to the sill and drop the five or six feet to the ground on the other side. But Dr. Isaacson's voice carried, and Emily stopped, startled by what she heard.

"Alice telephoned to tell me that you had requested the Carter file."

The other person in the office answered but was speaking softly, so Emily couldn't make out what was being said.

"No, she didn't deliberately open the file." As Dr. Isaacson spoke again, he sounded farther away, closer to his desk. "She accidentally dropped it. That's when she saw this photograph. She was as disturbed as I was at this photograph of a terrified child, so she copied the photo and sent it to me with her explanation. She knew that photo didn't belong in the Carter file, but she sent the entire file to you, as you had requested."

Again Emily strained to hear the other person, but she couldn't. Who was with Dr. Isaacson? Who had taken and kept her photograph?

"Yes, we can agree that it's Emily Wood," Dr. Isaacson said. "It couldn't be anyone else. But she had never been brought to the center by her parents. I would remember, even without referring to the records. However, since you state that you were not aware of the photograph's existence, and neither was I . . ."

There was more conversation, and Dr. Isaacson lowered his voice, no longer as disturbed as when he began, so Emily was unable to hear more than a snatch or two after he said, "Yes, I can see how the special problems with the Carter child could help you with the student you mentioned — both of them procrastinators."

Suddenly his voice was much closer, just outside the bathroom door. "Thank you for your time. The question is how that photograph got into the Carter file, but it's not something we can delve into at this time. I'd appreciate it if you wouldn't mention the existence of this photo to any of the other staff members. Sooner or later the explanation will turn up, and in the meantime we have important work to do here this summer."

Panicked, expecting the door to open at any second, Emily climbed onto the sink, boosted herself to the windowsill, and swung out, dropping and landing on her feet. She dove through the hibiscus bushes that hedged that side of the building and ran, not stopping until she reached the dining room.

Who had been in the office with Dr. Isaacson? Who had taken her photograph? It had to have been the person who had warned her eight years ago that she'd be found.

Emily accepted the loaded cafeteria tray that was handed to her, plopped it on the nearest table in the nearly empty room, and began to eat automatically, not having the slightest idea what she'd been served. She shouldn't have run. Or maybe she should have gone back to the hall to see who had left Dr. Isaacson's office. What was she doing here eating lunch?

What had she done with her notebook? For a moment she was so frightened she felt dizzy.

Emily took two deep breaths, trying to

steady herself so that she could think clearly. She pictured herself leaving Mrs. Comstock's room, notebook in hand. She had spoken with Dr. Bonaduce and Mrs. Hill, and her notebook? Yes, she'd been holding it at the time.

Then she had walked down the hall, had stopped at Dr. Isaacson's office and gone inside. The table . . . the little table by the door . . . she distinctly remembered putting her notebook on the table.

Had it been noticed? Had someone found it?

Shoving back her tray, Emily rushed through the dining room and lobby and down the hall.

This time she knocked at Dr. Isaacson's door and waited, terrified at the idea of coming face to face with him. But no one answered.

Again Emily knocked, a little more loudly, and when no one came she tried the knob. It turned easily, and the door opened.

Emily took just one step inside and stopped. Her heart beat faster, and she suddenly felt sick. Her notebook was gone.

"Is this yours?" A low voice spoke behind her.

Emily whirled, choking back a scream.

Dr. Hampton stood before her, Emily's

notebook in her outstretched hand. "Your name is on the cover," she said.

Too frightened to answer, Emily simply nodded, accepted the notebook, and clutched it to her chest.

Dr. Hampton's voice was calm and easy, but her gaze drilled into Emily. "You apparently left it on the table during your last appointment with Dr. Isaacson," she said.

"H-he didn't give it to you?" Emily managed to ask.

"No. I stopped by his office a little early, thinking he might be back from the staff meeting. I saw the notebook and thought I'd take it to the lunchroom to give to you."

"I didn't see you in the lunchroom," Emily whispered.

Dr. Hampton smiled. "You saved me the trip. I had just stepped into my office to get my handbag when I heard someone knock at Dr. Isaacson's door. I glanced out to see who it was, and luckily it was you."

"Well, uh . . . thank you," Emily said, glad that her voice was returning. She wondered if Dr. Hampton had looked through her notebook and seen the notes she'd written about her project, which included Dr. Hampton's name. It might be best to tell her as much as possible right now.

"For my English project I'm writing interviews with the staff members here at Camp Excel who were at the educational center when it opened in 1993," Emily said. "You and Dr. Anderson and Dr. Bonaduce and Mrs. Comstock and Mrs. Hill."

"And Dr. Isaacson, of course."

"Oh, yes. Dr. Isaacson."

Dr. Hampton's gaze seemed to deepen. "It's a fine project, but I'm afraid you'll have to leave me out," she said. "I didn't join the educational center until it had been well established."

"But —" Emily stopped short. Mr. Anderson had named Dr. Hampton among those who had been with the center from the start. Had he been mistaken? Or was she lying?

"Were you there eight years ago?" Emily asked.

"Closer to seven. And you?"

"Ei—" Emily quickly caught herself and said, "My parents never took me to the center. We live in Houston, not Dallas." As she had done so many times, she hunched her shoulders and ducked her head, letting her hair fall in front of her face. *Is she the one?* Emily wondered.

"There you are, Emily. We've been waiting and *waiting* for you."

Emily straightened, pushed back her hair,

and saw Taylor standing next to Dr. Hampton. Maxwell was right behind her.

"I forgot my notebook," Emily said. As she began to edge around Dr. Hampton, she said, "Thanks again for getting my notebook back to me. I'll see you at my session tomorrow morning."

"Sooner than that," Dr. Hampton said.

Maxwell added, "Dr. Hampton's going with us to tour the cave. I saw her name on the sign-up sheet."

"I wouldn't miss it," Dr. Hampton answered, her eyes still on Emily.

"Um . . . great," Emily said.

She tried not to flinch as Dr. Hampton gave her a quick pat on the shoulder and returned to her office.

"Hurry up, Emily," Taylor said. "Put on your swimsuit. Coach Jinks has got kayaks lined up on the beach. It looks like fun."

Coach Jinks, the hair on his muscular legs bleached to a golden sheen over his tan, pranced up and down the short beach in front of the kayaks, beaming at the campers who were clustered around the narrow boats. "Today we're going to try out the kayaks," he said. "If they don't sink we'll use them to hold kayak races."

Nobody laughed, but he didn't seem to

care. "You can all swim, right?"

No one disagreed, so he went on. "Wear life vests anyway. The current out there can be strong, and I feel lazy this afternoon. I don't want to play lifeguard."

He counted off a dozen of the swimmers standing closest to the water, who included Emily and Taylor, and handed them life vests. "Pick your kayaks, push them out into the water till they float, and climb in. Watch what you do with the paddles so you don't accidentally clobber your neighbors. And don't go too far. Be back in twenty minutes so the next group can have a turn."

Emily climbed into a red kayak with a bright yellow number thirteen on the nose. Unlucky number? Or lucky? As she glided out into the deeper water, the little boat sailed smoothly. The hot afternoon sun gilded the water that rippled in a fan along both sides of the kayak, and the steady rhythm of the double paddle as it dipped and rose was hypnotizing. Emily relaxed, loving the motion, loving the water.

She glanced back at the shore, surprised that the people on the beach had shrunk to tiny stick figures. "Don't go too far," the coach had said, so Emily swung her kayak in an arc to the right. She'd head upstream for a while and circle back.

The beach was soon out of sight, and she looked for familiar landmarks. There was the little dock, a rowboat still tied to one of the posts. There was only a small break in the thick forest and shrubbery that crowded to the water's edge. From her spot out on the water Emily couldn't detect the path she had taken.

She steered the kayak closer to shore, drawn to this secret spot that could have meant Taylor's death . . . or her own. One of the fat gulls that frequented the lake sat motionless on the left post that supported the dock, its beady, black eyes trained on Emily.

"Don't be afraid of me. I won't disturb you," Emily whispered to the bird.

Suddenly Emily was aware of the *slap-drip* of a paddle and saw that another kayak had swung in beside her. She glanced up to see Taylor, who was leaning forward, squinting to get a good look at the dock.

"Who is that near the dock?" Taylor asked.

Emily caught a flash of movement in the woods, but whoever or whatever it was disappeared behind the trunk of a thick oak. "I couldn't tell," she said.

"I couldn't either, except I think it was a woman."

"What makes you think so?" Emily asked.

"I'm not sure. Her clothes? Her hair? No. Maybe it was the way she moved."

As they drew nearer to the dock, Emily backpaddled, stopping the forward movement of her kayak. Taylor did the same. Silently their boats bobbed up and down in the water, the only sounds on the lake the whispery slaps of water against the kayaks. In the still, hot air not a single leaf moved.

"Do you want to tie up to the dock and get out?" Taylor spoke loudly, her voice carrying over the water.

Emily turned to Taylor to answer, so she didn't see what happened. She only heard a crack, like rock hitting wood. With a loud squawk, the gull shot up from the dock, wings flapping, and sailed just over their heads.

Taylor let out a surprised yell, waved her arms at the bird, and nearly lost her balance.

"Go!" Emily shouted. "Get away from here!" She paddled frantically, trying to turn her kayak around. At the same time she kept looking over her shoulder. Whoever had startled the bird could have easily slipped from her hiding place back into the woods . . . or she could have remained where she had been, watching them.

Desperately, Emily fumbled with her

204

paddle, nearly dropping it, until finally her kayak shot out into the lake, away from the dock, following Taylor's kayak. Emily paddled furiously, breathing in short, desperate gasps. Although she had seen no one, she felt the presence of whoever was in the forest. It seemed to be reaching toward her with the terrible, evil grasp of Loki.

CHAPTER 22

How dare she!

Emily Wood is haunting me. She broke into my place of solitude. She interrupted the little time I have left to quietly and efficiently review the plans I have made.

Well, very soon she will no longer be either an irritant or a danger to me.

It's time to act.

CHAPTER 23

At four o'clock Emily climbed into one of the vans with Haley, Maxwell, and Taylor, whose eyes were again rimmed with smudged black eyeliner. With them were some of the others from the two history classes, and Coach Jinks, who was driving.

He turned on the ignition, but before he pulled out onto the drive he twisted around to grin at his passengers in the back and middle seats. "When you're down in the cave, watch out for the crazies," he said.

"What crazies?" Taylor asked. Emily, who was sitting next to her, could feel her tense.

"The ones who live there," Coach said. "They're all bats."

A couple of people groaned.

"Get it?" Coach asked. "Bats . . . crazies." He swung onto the road and headed west.

Haley made a face of disgust and said, "It's going to be a complete waste of time going into a place that has bats living in it."

Taylor's voice shook as she said, "I just wish the cave were out in the open and not underground."

Maxwell snickered. "Someday, when I'm a famous playwright, I'll remember this inane dialogue and use it in one of my plays."

"Good for you," Haley said. "Then Dr. Weil's classes can diagram your sentences."

Some of the people in the van laughed, but Maxwell tugged his cap more snugly over his ears and slid down in his seat, his knees nearly up to his chin.

Emily, at his right side, bent to speak quietly to him. "You deserved that," she said. "You shouldn't have made fun of Haley and Taylor. They're your friends."

He muttered, "When I'm famous —" but Emily interrupted.

"How about now?" she asked. "Who are you now?"

Maxwell turned to glare at her, but she asked, "What have you written? What are you writing *now?*"

He sputtered, little bubbles of spit appearing at the corners of his mouth. "You don't know what it's like being a playwright."

"That's right," she admitted. "I've never written a play, and I bet you haven't, either."

For a moment, Maxwell's mouth hung open. "But I'm going to," he said.

"Why don't you try writing one now?"

"I'm too young. I haven't had enough life experiences," he said. "The people who publish plays wouldn't take me seriously."

"You wouldn't have to send your play to a publisher," Emily told him. "You could write for practice, or just because you want to. Don't writers have to learn how to follow all the rules before they write for publication?"

Maxwell's forehead wrinkled as he thought. "I haven't lived an exciting life. I really haven't done anything. What would I write about?"

"Write about your family. Maybe in your play they could all realize how they had misjudged your main character after he bravely saved a girl's life."

"And they'd be sorry."

"Sure, if that's the way you want to write it."

Maxwell sat up straighter in his seat. "You're telling me I can't talk about being a playwright. I just have to be one."

"Something like that," Emily answered.

He spoke almost in a whisper. "But what if I try writing a play and find I can't do it?"

Emily touched his hand gently. "On the

other hand, what if you try writing a play and find it's even better than you thought it might be?"

Maxwell's eyes widened. "I'll think about it," he said, and turned to stare out the window.

Haley leaned across Taylor to tell Emily, "I wish you had drawn a rune this morning. It's bad enough to have to waste time wandering through a cave, I shouldn't have to worry about you while I'm doing it."

"What makes you think I'll be in any more danger inside a cave than out of it?" Emily asked.

Haley gave her a sharp look. "Do you have your potion with you?"

Emily automatically touched the pocket of her shirt and felt the small vial under her fingertips. "Yes," she said.

Haley drew back, satisfied. "Good. Then you'll be protected."

Impatiently, Emily answered, "How can you believe that a little bottle of black inky stuff can —"

"It was inspired by Loki and verified by the *curandero*," Haley said smugly.

"This is the real world we live in, not some weird place run by magic stones and people who claim to foretell the future. I don't understand —"

"That's exactly it," Haley interrupted. "There's a great deal about the mystical side of life that you *don't* understand."

"Longhorn Cavern coming up," Coach called out as the van bounced into a narrow side road.

Emily felt Taylor stiffen.

"It's going to be okay," Emily whispered to Taylor, but Taylor looked as terrified as the young Emily had looked in the photograph. Emily shivered. How could she help Taylor when she couldn't even help herself?

Some of the vans had already arrived, and within a few minutes the last two pulled into the parking lot next to the administration building with its sturdy stone walls. Some of the teachers had come with the group, among them Dr. Weil.

Firmly holding Taylor's hand, Emily walked to the spot where everyone was gathering.

"Line up, line up. First group, follow Dr. Hampton," Mrs. Comstock called. She pointed, waving a small sprig of honeysuckle. "Go through the building and down the path to the entrance to the cave."

As Maxwell was herded reluctantly with those sent ahead, Mrs. Comstock sent some of the other kids in a group with Coach Jinks, Dr. Anderson, and Dr. Weil.

Emily stepped forward with Taylor but found Mrs. Comstock in her way. "There's no need to rush," Mrs. Comstock said. "Stick with me."

As they walked into the building, Emily saw a gift shop to her left and a sunny room with a snack bar, tables, and chairs to her right.

Taylor blurted out, "Mrs. Comstock, I could stay here and wait for you. I wouldn't mind."

Mrs. Comstock moved to put an arm around Taylor's shoulders, separating her from Emily. "You're going to love the cavern," she said. "It's really impressive. Just wait until you see it."

As they left the building and started down the path and steps that led to the cave's entrance, Mrs. Comstock glanced back at Emily. "There's nothing to be afraid of in the cave. No one's ever been lost there . . . yet."

Emily gulped and stumbled, grabbing for the handrail. Had Mrs. Comstock meant that as a warning?

Maxwell was out of sight, and Emily had lost track of Haley. Where was Haley?

Glancing ahead, Emily saw that the steps seemed to descend into a black hole, but as she came closer, out of the glare of the sun, she saw that the entrance to the cave was lighted with hidden, recessed lamps.

The group from Camp Excel swarmed into the entrance room, passing a barred iron gate with a padlock swinging from the lock. The gate had been opened wide and pushed to one side.

Taylor stopped so suddenly that Emily nearly plowed into her. Taylor pointed at the gate. Her voice trembling, she asked Mrs. Comstock, "We aren't going to be locked in, are we?"

"Of course not," Mrs. Comstock assured her. "That gate is only shut and locked during nighttime hours, when the cave isn't open to the public. It's to keep vandals out, not keep people in."

Slowly Emily descended the rough stone steps into a room that was noticeably cooler than the hot afternoon temperature outside. A short, plump woman in a park ranger's uniform glanced over the group, then raised her voice, calling them to pay attention.

"I know that your teacher has probably talked to you about the history of the formation of the cavern and how it eventually drained into the Colorado River. I'll be repeating some of what she said, and I'm going to point out special features of each room as we walk through them, but first we've got to go over a few rules.

"Stay on the paths. No pushing or shoving. Some places are slippery, and you could easily fall. Water still drains from the cave, and at the edges of some of the paths you'll see little rivulets and even pools. There are a few drops, such as the Wishing Well, which is a drainage pit leading into lower caverns."

Someone interrupted. "Do you mean there are caverns underneath the Longhorn Cavern?"

The ranger nodded. "There is a large area intertwined with caves. We think it covers hundreds of miles. Many caves haven't been discovered yet, and many are too difficult to explore. We do have a special tour on Saturdays, when we take visitors to sections of the cavern below the normal tour. It's a strenuous, rugged trip that takes close to three hours, and you'll have to rent special safety equipment to take it. Also, you can plan on getting muddy and wet."

Taylor gave a little moan and reached out again for Emily's hand, gripping it tightly.

"We aren't going to go there," Emily whispered. "We'll be walking on paths."

"But we'll be underground," Taylor cried out. As a few people turned around to look at her, her voice rose. "I don't want to be underground!"

"I'll be right here with you," Mrs. Comstock said.

The ranger shook her head. "If she's claustrophobic it's better that she wait for you in the snack bar. We'll have to bend over double and walk for a long stretch as we pass under the low ceiling of Lumbago Alley, and she'll panic."

A girl near the front turned and began to squeeze toward them. "I'll stay with her!" she called out. "I'm claustrophobic, too."

Dr. Anderson stepped up to Mrs. Comstock. "I'll go with the girls," she said. With her arms around their shoulders she shepherded them to the stairway. Within minutes they were out of sight.

The ranger said, "Everyone stick together. This is a large group, and we can't keep counting noses. As I turn on the lights ahead of us, I'll turn off the lights in the rooms we leave. We don't want anyone left in the dark."

She paused only a moment, then said, "Everyone ready? Okay. Take another good look at the large hole that formed the cavern's present entrance. This came about when part of the ceiling of this room collapsed."

Clattering down the steps, Haley burst into the entrance room. "Sorry I'm late," she said to Mrs. Comstock. "They had the most wonderful polished-rock jewelry in the gift shop. I mean, I just had to get a pair of earrings. And then I —"

"If you'll please quiet down back there," the ranger interrupted, "I'll finish my explanation." She waited, eyes boring into Haley's, until Haley squirmed. Then she went on. "On our tour we'll make a long loop, traveling through a number of rooms, all the way to what we call Rock of a Million Layers. Then we'll retrace our steps back a short way until we turn off on the other side of the loop. Our tour will end back in this spot. We'll travel through the crystal rooms first. They consist of two passageways that form a loop on either side of the main trail. We like to call them Crystal City because the walls are encrusted with large crystalline masses of calcite, which gleam like crystal in the light."

She stepped ahead, touching a switch that had been hidden in the wall, and the first room of the cave burst into a wild pattern of glitter and shadows.

The ranger went on to explain about pools of calcium-saturated water, but Emily became lost in her own thoughts. Maxwell was somewhere ahead. Taylor had left the cave. And Haley had moved on to join two of the other girls who were all busy trying on the pendant and earrings Haley had bought in the gift shop. For the moment Emily was on her own.

Maybe I should leave the cave, too, she thought. *There's still time.* She glanced back to the bend, around which was the entrance to the cave, then turned, taking two steps toward it, before Mrs. Comstock grabbed her arm and pulled her to a stop.

"Taylor will be all right. Someone's with her," she said, and Emily found herself being tugged around and pulled toward the group, which had begun following the ranger.

"I've decided I don't want to go through the cave," Emily said.

"Nonsense. It's a marvelous experience," Mrs. Comstock insisted.

"But —"

Mrs. Comstock's voice became firm. "No excuses, Emily," she said. She thrust the sprig of honeysuckle at her. "Here. Take this. Isn't the fragrance heavenly? Somehow this pale little flower reminds me of you."

Emily shivered, wishing Mrs. Comstock would let go of her arm. Was the honeysuckle a message, too? Emily wondered if

Mrs. Comstock was aware of the honeysuckle in the photograph and this was her way of telling her. That would mean that Mrs. Comstock was the one who had called to her and threatened to find her.

Emily knew she couldn't accuse Mrs. Comstock to either Dr. Isaacson or the police. She still had no proof. Emily fingered the vial of potion in her pocket.

Suddenly Mrs. Comstock released her. "Come along," she said. "We have to keep up with the others."

The ranger paused and pointed out a formation called the Queen's Watchdog, in which limestone had naturally eroded into the shape of a dog, and the Queen's Throne, a massive flowstone. Above and around them the striped, layered walls were scooped and gouged out in impressive whorls and surrealistic carvings. Emily felt as if she were floating in an unreal world without time or meaning.

The group turned to the right, entering a narrow stretch the ranger said was called Lovers' Lane. Emily reluctantly trailed the group, trying to stay as far away from Mrs. Comstock as possible. She jumped as the lights turned off in the room they had left, plunging it into total blackness, and scurried to keep up with the rest, who were listening to the ranger's description of the history of the cave. But she couldn't keep from glancing over her shoulder at the dark mouth that seemed to be swallowing their footprints.

To Emily's surprise, she thought she saw a small, wavering light moving through the darkness. She blinked and looked again, but it had disappeared.

The group filed through one of the narrow bends, Emily at the rear. Again she looked back. Again she spotted the light, which seemed to be following them.

This time the small beam didn't turn off, and as it came closer, Emily could see that it was Dr. Anderson, carrying a flashlight. As she walked toward Emily into the lighted alley, she smiled and said, "I thought I'd meet up with you sooner." She turned off her flashlight and held it down at her side.

"How did you know where we'd be?" Emily asked.

"I've been here before. I know the route."

Emily realized she could no longer hear the ranger's voice and there was no sign of the others on the tour. "We'd better hurry and catch up," she said.

"We've got time," Dr. Anderson said calmly. "In fact, this gives us a good chance to talk, Emily. I know that something is bothering you. Would you like to tell me about it?"

"Not now," Emily said. She began edging down the path. "If they turn out the lights . . ."

At that moment the lane was suddenly smothered in total darkness. "They don't know we're here!" Emily cried. She took a step and stumbled against the rough wall, nearly falling. "Help!" she tried to yell, but her voice wobbled and was weak.

"They can't hear you," Dr. Anderson said. "By now they're in the Indian Council Room." Calmly she explained, "Lovers' Lane makes two sharp turns. We're at the back of the loop, and sound won't carry as far as the Council Room."

The voice! Emily thought. In the darkness, Dr. Anderson's voice stood out, and she remembered it well. Her heart beat faster, and her hands began to sweat. She wiped them on her shorts, fighting the panic that made her want to scream. She put her hands to her face, but the dark was so deep she couldn't even see the shape of her fingers. She thought she heard whispers and something skittering through the pebbles near her feet. "Turn on your flashlight!" she cried.

"When I'm ready," Dr. Anderson said. A

scolding note came into her voice as she complained, "You didn't come when I called you. I said, 'Little girl, come back,' but you didn't."

Emily gasped, pressing up against the cold rock wall. "If I had, you would have killed me, too."

"So you saw and heard it all. You knew. Everything."

"You said you'd come looking for me. You told me you'd find me."

"I tried my best. I was sure you must live in Dallas, and I scoured the nearby neighborhoods."

Emily groaned. She remembered Dr. Anderson asking her parents at the reception how long they had lived in Dallas. She should have realized that Dr. Anderson had remembered her. Right that minute she should have known.

"My career has always meant everything to me," Dr. Anderson said. "My position at the educational center was my dream come true. The only way to get it was to falsify my credentials. No one would have known. No one would have cared. My work was impeccable. When Amelia Foxworth told me she had investigated and discovered the truth and would make my actions public, I reacted out of fear. Don't you understand?

She would have ruined my career, my entire future, but I didn't plan to kill her. I just reacted."

Emily, still flattened against the wall, took a hesitant step to the left, away from the sound of Dr. Anderson's voice. Something seemed to brush against her cheek, and she shuddered, trying to swat it away, but her fingers touched only the cold air in the cave. She reached with her toes for solid footing but couldn't find it. Where was she? Swallowed up by this inky darkness, she had no sense of direction.

"Please turn on your flashlight!" she begged.

"Have you been listening to me?" Dr. Anderson demanded. "Do you understand how I must continue to protect the outstanding reputation I've built for myself?"

Desperately, Emily tried to remember what her surroundings had looked like. Did the trail curve to the left? The right? Was there a drop to one side? The intense blackness that pressed against her eyes was terrifying.

"Answer me! Don't you understand?" Dr. Anderson's voice rose in a screech.

"You killed Dr. Foxworth," Emily said.

"I told you why. I didn't choose to have her die. And I hope you realize that I have no choice in what I'm about to do now." Dr. Anderson's voice grew calmer and more determined. "Just to our right there's a rise some people try to climb on, even though they're not supposed to. They'll find your body below it. They'll assume that you climbed and fell. I left the girls in the snack bar, fortified with Cokes and sandwiches, and told them I was going to step outside and look around. They think I'm with them. They'll say I was when they're asked."

Emily tried to step in the opposite direction. She was determined to move so she wouldn't be an easy target. But her foot dislodged some pebbles that clattered as they rolled. She had no weapon. Nothing with which to defend herself.

"You aren't going to escape, so don't bother trying," Dr. Anderson said quietly.

I do have a weapon, Emily thought, remembering. Her breath coming in short gasps, her heart racing, she reached for the vial of potion in her pocket. Carefully she pulled out the little stopper and placed her thumb securely over the open top of the vial. Her thumb stung where the liquid touched it.

Suddenly the bright beam of Dr. Anderson's flashlight was aimed directly at Emily's face, blinding her.

Instead of ducking or trying to get away, Emily moved forward, toward the light. With her left hand she grabbed the flashlight, shoving it to one side. Now she could see Dr. Anderson's face, strained with anger, and the hand clutching the rock that was raised high over her head.

Emily twisted to the right just as the rock came down, painfully scraping her left shoulder. Pulling back her thumb, Emily threw the contents of the vial directly into Dr. Anderson's eyes.

Dr. Anderson screamed, let go of the flashlight, and bent double, clawing at her face.

Suddenly, the recessed lighting flashed on. Haley ran down the path toward Emily, Coach Jinks and Dr. Weil behind her.

"When I realized you weren't with us, I told Coach —," Haley began. She gasped. "What happened to Dr. Anderson?"

Emily watched Dr. Anderson, on her knees at the side of the path, scooping water from a little stream and splashing it into her eyes.

"She'll be all right," Emily explained. "I had to stop her. She tried to kill me because I saw her push Dr. Foxworth over the stairs near the pool at the educational center."

"What! Is this true?" Dr. Weil took Dr.

Anderson by her shoulders and pulled her to her feet.

Haley gasped again as she saw the empty vial Emily held out to her. "The potion!" she said triumphantly. "You used the potion!"

"It was the only way I had to defend myself."

Mrs. Comstock and Dr. Hampton appeared, their eyes wide with astonishment. Maxwell pushed forward, along with some of the others.

Dr. Anderson babbled, "Dr. Foxworth knew! I had to stop her! I didn't mean to kill her! It wasn't my fault. And Emily saw what happened! She was going to tell!"

To Emily's relief, Dr. Weil calmly took charge. He soothed Dr. Anderson, trying to quiet her. Then he sent two girls back to the administration building to call the sheriff's department, and he picked out Maxwell and Coach Jinks to assist Dr. Anderson from the cave.

Before they left, while everyone seemed to be talking at once, Maxwell turned to Emily, pushing the knitted edge of his cap back from his forehead. "You're right about what I should do," he said. "I'm going to try my hand at writing. I'll call it *Maxwell McLaren, The Early Years*. I'll be able to write it, won't I, Emily?"

"Yes," Emily said. "I think you will."

As Maxwell and Coach Jinks disappeared around a bend in the path, Haley asked, "Em, do you think there's a chance Max really will be famous someday?"

Emily shrugged and answered, "Who knows? At least he's going to find out if he really can write."

Dr. Hampton stepped forward, Mrs. Comstock elbowing her way to a place beside her.

"Emily, I don't understand," Dr. Hampton said. "If you thought you were in trouble, why didn't you come to me for help?"

"You lied to me about when you came to work at the center," Emily said. "You were there when it opened, and you said you weren't."

Dr. Hampton looked surprised. "I didn't think it mattered. I was there only the first semester. Then I returned to where I had been employed to finish a project on which I was needed."

"I needed the truth," Emily told her. "You didn't give it to me."

Mrs. Comstock smiled sympathetically as she moved forward. "You could have come to me, dear," she said. "I tried to assure you that you could always confide in me."

"You tried too hard," Emily said.

The cold, damp walls of the cave seemed to press toward her, and she could hear a scurrying sound coming from the dark shadows. Bats? Mice?

"I want out of this place," Emily said.

Haley grasped Emily's arm and steered her back down the path in the direction of the entrance. "I'll go with you," she said. "We'll find Taylor and tell her everything that happened."

She paused, turning Emily to face her. "*I'll* be the one to tell her. After all, it was Loki who warned you, and it was the *curandero*'s potion that saved you." Her smile was smug. "All because of me."

Emily didn't argue. She knew she'd be repeating the entire story to Dr. Isaacson, to the police, to her parents, and to countless other people before it was over.

Unfortunately, she thought, *it will never be over.* Nightmares had a way of returning when least expected, and now the old dreams would be joined by a new one: the haunted eyes of a desperate woman in a dark cave.

But Emily realized she was no longer afraid to be Emily. She no longer needed to be invisible. She smiled at Haley. "I can handle it," she said.

"Well, of course," Haley said.

Emily followed Haley from the cave up the steps into the late-afternoon sunlight.

About the Author

Joan Lowery Nixon has been called the grande dame of young adult mysteries and is the author of more than 130 books for young readers, including *The Trap*; *The Making of a Writer*; *Playing for Keeps*; *Ghost Town*; *Nobody's There*; *Who Are You?*; *The Haunting*; *Murdered, My Sweet*; *Don't Scream*; *Spirit Seeker*; *The Dark and Deadly Pool*; *Shadowmaker*; *The Weekend Was* Murder!; and *Search for the Shadowman*. Joan Lowery Nixon is the only four-time winner of the Edgar Allan Poe Best Young Adult Mystery Award. She received the award for *The Kidnapping of Christina Lattimore*, *The Séance*, *The Name of the Game Was Murder*, and *The Other Side of Dark*, which also won the California Young Reader Medal. Her historical fiction includes the award-winning series The Orphan Train Adventures, Orphan Train Children, and Colonial Williamsburg: Young Americans.

The employees of Thorndike Press hope you have enjoyed this Large Print book. All our Thorndike and Wheeler Large Print titles are designed for easy reading, and all our books are made to last. Other Thorndike Press Large Print books are available at your library, through selected bookstores, or directly from us.

For information about titles, please call:

(800) 223-1244

or visit our Web site at:

www.gale.com/thorndike
www.gale.com/wheeler

To share your comments, please write:

Publisher
Thorndike Press
295 Kennedy Memorial Drive
Waterville, ME   04901